THE PRESENCE
BETWEEN

An Untouchable Love

CORINNE ARROWOOD

Published by Corinne Arrowood
United States of America
www.corinnearrowood.com

ISBN: 979-8-9873642-0-8 (eBook)
ISBN: 979-8-9873642-1-5 (Trade Paperback)
ISBN: 979-8-9873642-2-2 (Hardcover)

Cover and Interior Design by Cyrusfiction Productions.

Contents

The House Hurstall

"I hate this wretched country and its Neanderthal population. I want to go back home. Please, to the heavens above, make them reconsider this tragic decision." She was absolutely precious and extremely precocious. I could listen to her constant stream of colorful chatter forever. From the moment I laid eyes on Miss Devon Hurstall, I must admit I was smitten. Her bouncing mahogany ringlets framed her angelic peaches and cream complexion—a real-life porcelain doll. Beautiful violet eyes twinkled beneath a fringe of thick black lashes. She was sheer perfection in the sassiest kind of way, but all I could do was silently observe.

Stomp. Stomp. Stomp. Devon made her way up the staircase to her bedchamber. I knew what was to happen next. A loud bang would reverberate through the grand old home as she slammed her door closed with every ounce of strength and disapproval she could muster.

"Charlotte, I mean it this time," she spoke to the lifeless stuffed bear propped up on a stack of gingham and eyelet pillows. "If Mummy and Father continue to refuse to move back to Chelsea and civilization, I am going to run away. Certainly, Grandmother would book my flight home and allow me to live with her. I could return to the Childers School for Girls and resume right where I left off. They would be elated upon my arrival. I

1

will warn Mummy and Father one more time. They will be tremendously sorrowful when I move back to England. Father should never have taken the position here and moved us to this horrific place."

Such idle threats from this dramatic child were delightful. I supposed I had not taken her sadness seriously; I only wished I could soothe her homesick heart.

New Orleans was, in truth, about as different to Chelsea as our North had been to The South during the days of The Civil War. While there was an undeniable charm to the quaint city, it lacked the antiquity and sophistication of Devon's homeland. I understood her torment and sadness as I, too, had felt an awkwardness when I first came to live in this strange city. Boston had far more couth, at least in my young, jaded mind.

Mother's voice carried into the room from the bottom of the staircase, "Devon dear, you must come down. Father is home and requires your presence in the lounge." Laura's voice was soft, delicate as though of royal birth. While sweet and lovely, she was not one to defy.

The angelic face contorted as Devon glared in the direction of the door. "What do you think would happen if I refused?" She asked of her stuffed bear friend. "My thoughts, exactly, Charlotte!" Scattering her pillows from the bed, she quickly grabbed Charlotte and climbed beneath the covers. Feigning sleep, what a darling attempt at rebellion.

Again, with a little more impatience, Mother's voice beckoned, "Devon dear, Father wants to see you in the lounge. Come down straight away." A minute passed before soft footsteps whispered upon the staircase treads. I didn't think my precious princess would pull the wool over her mother's eyes. Quietly the door opened. Mother stood still with her arms folded. From her expression, I derived Mother was not amused.

I expected her to turn on her heel with an angry command, but to my surprise, she dramatically flung the covers back and tickled Devon. I had sensations of what once was warmth and happiness hearing the giggles. "Mummy, I wanted to fool you, but you are ever so smart as not to be fooled." While the atmosphere was jolly, my rascally adoration managed to form the perfect pout face with her puckered rose-colored lips, the bottom lip jutting out just enough. "Mummy, do I have to talk to Father? He can be grumpy, you know."

"Come along." Mother smoothed Devon's mussed hair. "Young lady, Father does not like to be kept waiting." Even I knew the man's determined ways. "Resist your temptation of surliness, dear. The only one gleaning anything from such is you. Devon, remember your manners and stand up straight. Best foot forward." Mother and Father were rigid to a fault. Sometimes they appeared void of emotion, yet there was the odd moment of play which I relished for Miss Devon.

The lounge was dramatic, with draperies swept to the side and cascading into puddles on the floor. Father sat with his legs crossed, nose deep into a newspaper. I peered over his shoulder. Hardly a surprise; it was always the financials. He rarely had time for playful affection. Laura cleared her throat. He lowered his reading, folded it perfectly in half, and then placed it on the table next to him.

"Good evening, Devon. I trust all went accordingly at school?" He uncrossed his legs. It would have been an opportune moment for a cuddle. Father patted his lap, and my essence leapt with joy. Her sweet lips turned into a smile perfect as a bow. Her dimples were only outdone by her glistening eyes. "Devon, nothing would make me happier than a cuddle from you." Gleefully, she climbed, without haste, into his lap. One would think it was the picture of love as Laura drew close. "Mother tells me you've been sad today. Is that so, and what has made you sad?"

I couldn't help but think, *oh sir, please don't open the garden gate*; nonetheless, what was done was done. My precocious young friend seemed never to be at a loss for words—chatty, opinionated creature, my Devon.

The bottom lip jutted forward again. She held his face and looked with sternness, her brow crinkling into a frown. "Father, the children at school are imbeciles. They can barely read, and when it is my turn, they snicker. The Mistress loves my reading. After I read, she compliments me." Her arched eyebrows displayed a happy appearance of accomplishment with a splash of continued disgust.

"And?" He cocked his head in curiosity. "To me, I would think it would make you feel happy. Not so?" He smiled at her. I knew he loved her with every heartbeat, but sometimes he needlessly was too stoic, as though anything else was unacceptable behavior for a man. If he only knew, as I learned all too well, he'd come to regret and long for these days once she slipped from his control. Although I must admit, reining or controlling Miss Devon was a contradiction in itself. At the tender age of eight, she was already her own person – sometimes a most challenging person.

She puffed up her chest and squared her eyes with an explosive sigh. She meant business. I knew the look. "No!" Father's eyes widened with amusement; dare he not laugh, oh no. "Jeffrey, the boy who sits behind me, pulls my hair and jeers at me. He calls me 'smarty pants' and 'show off.' The last name was the teacher's pet! How dare he. Just because he's a baboon doesn't give him the go-ahead to call me names. He's even worse than a baboon, and he smells bad. Stinky like the play yard dirt."

It's in those times I wanted to tell her to give ol' Jeffrey a few years. The boy would wish he could touch her hair or have her attention, and she would be ever-so inclined to accept his playfulness. Alas, the trials of growing up. Father raised his eyebrows. "Did you actually call this young man a baboon?" I could see him holding back a chuckle.

She jumped off his lap and stood proudly before him. Shoulders back, her posture was positively rigid. "I most certainly did!" She made gestures like dusting her hands. She was done and most proud of herself.

Mother, who had been silent, chimed in, "Devon, ladies do not name call. Name-calling shows a lack of vocabulary or anything more intelligent to say. You think you won, but I'm afraid you stooped to his level. Ignore his words and rise above." Mother quite often forgot what being a child looked or felt like.

4

Oh dear, she flashed her eyes at her mother with an outward cockiness bordering on flippancy. "Next time," she batted her eyes, "I will merely say I feel sorry for him. Obviously, he is a vocabulary-challenged baboon!"

Father softly chuckled. Mother sent a scolding look regarding the breach. "Ian, you're not helping. Must you?" I spotted a slight twinkle in Mother's eye and an upturned twitch to the corners of her lips. I felt a sense of joy leap within me; how delightful. Admittedly, Mother and Father had a rather strange relationship at best. They were both too vested in formality, rarely shedding the façade.

The week drew to an end. Devon had annoyed Mother and Father with her insistent whine about returning to England. At one point, Mother stomped her foot, pointed up the stairs, and sent my precious little friend to her room as punishment. If only Mother and Father could see what the darling had up her sleeve, they may have rescinded the sentence. Sitting Charlotte on a pillow, Devon began her whispered rant. "Charlotte, I told you, I feared it would come to this. Mummy and Father brought this whole mess upon themselves to use Mother's favorite expression to me."

In a mocking tone, with both hands on her hips, she continued, "'Devon, dear, don't try to put the blame on anyone else. You have brought this situation on yourself.' Charlotte, they are useless when it comes to listening to me. If they would merely take the time to explain their actions, but no, I'm just a child and do not require an explanation." A single tear tumbled from her eye. How I wished I could console her and explain that adults sometimes had to make unpleasant decisions.

Mother should at least let the child know that she, too, did not find this move to America particularly satisfying. I had seen Mother sobbing into her pillow a handful of times, at least. I had also heard one side of her conversation with a relative complaining about the change in their lives and how there was nothing she wouldn't give to return to England. Perhaps, Devon might find an ally in Mother, someone she could confide in; but that was not to be the case. The child had just been dismissed and punished for her feelings. *Tsk, tsk, Mother.* I shook my head in disgust.

5

Devon went down for dinner whence called and remained utterly silent throughout the meal. Once dismissed from the table, she returned to the bedchamber, climbed into bed, and fell asleep with Charlotte, the stuffed bear.

Saturday morning, my treasure woke before the sun came up. I curiously watched as she methodically emptied her school satchel of books, pads of paper, and writing implements. As quickly as she had cleared out the bag, she began stuffing it with her favorite nightdress, two carefully chosen ensembles, a hairbrush, and toiletries. Pondering with her finger, lightly tapping her chin, and forming a most calculating countenance, I observed her examine her room. With a sudden gleam, she grabbed her coat, mittens, and scarf and tucked them away inside her now travel bag.

"I believe that's everything, Charlotte," she muttered, then slid the bag beneath the bed. "First mission accomplished. I warned them, did I not? I thought you'd agree." She tip-toed down the stairs to the kitchen, climbed up on a stool, and picked up the telephone. I could hear the tone change with each number she pressed. It was almost melodic.

After Grandmother answered the call, she whispered, "Grandmother, it's Devon." She became silent for a moment, then replied, "I must be most quiet as not to wake Mummy and Father. Could you please purchase a ticket for me to come home? I could live with you, and I promise to listen to you. I could return to The Childer's Sch—" Devon listened for a moment. "I've tried to tell them, Grandmother, but they won't listen. They simply ignore me because I am a child, and what do I know." Her sweet little whisper gained force. "I am tired of them not listening and shushing me. I want to live with you. America is such an awful place, and the children are imbeciles. They can't even read without sounding out each letter like babies. You wouldn't believe it. Also, they are not very nice to me." I heard her voice hitch as the tears began to fall. She listened, and I saw as her head fell into her chest. "I understand, Grandmother. It's okay, and I still love you, but could you please talk to them? Pleeease." She ended the conversation and hung up, sniffling all the way to her bedchamber.

Quiet Observations

I observed with trepidation as Father Time rolled one year on to the next, as though merely turning the pages of a book. I didn't want my treasure to mature too fast. The time would come when she, too, would leave home. There had been many to come and go, but none as special as this sweet blossom.

The day ticked on, and excitement mounted. Before the front door opened, the laughter and squeals of eight young ladies, more like hyenas, could be heard throughout the house. This bombardment of the Hurstall's home was in celebration of Miss Devon's twelfth birthday. Oh, the verbosity and piercing sounds those young ladies made even rattled my soul. I knew I might be a tad prejudiced, but anyone with eyes and ears could tell that Devon was a class above the others.

Mother attempted to gather them for an early dinner, then the customary birthday song with cake and ice cream, but it simply was maddening, like herding cats. She managed, and as soon as all were seated, Mother rang a small handbell. She cleared her throat. "Devon, dear, there is a special surprise for your birthday. You must close your eyes without a peek. Ready?"

I knew the surprise and could hardly wait. Hope of hope, the reveal would be every bit as exciting as I had thought it would be, but one never knew with Miss Devon.

"Open your eyes!" Mother exclaimed.

When she opened them, Grandmother kissed her cheek. "Happy Birthday, my love."

It was the first time I'd seen tears of joy from Devon's violet eyes, and my soul filled. I'm certain there had been other times outside of this house, but it was my first experience, and what a splendid display of affection.

"Grandmother," she quickly rose from her seat for a long and loving embrace. "When did you arrive?" It was as though they were the only two souls in the room. Everyone and everything else paled.

"My sweetheart, your mother did a good job keeping me hidden until this moment. Of course, I wanted to see you when you first arrived from school. It was almost more than I could bear. The mere excitement created bubbles in my tummy, and I was absolutely nervous for time to pass." The love and affection emanated from Grandmother. Mother and Father loved Devon from the deepest part of their beings, but their demeanor was far less demonstrative, almost absent at times.

Miss Devon was the picture of her grandmother some fifty years prior. Grandmother's mahogany hair had streaks of silver entwined throughout her perfectly coiffed hair, pinned up in the tradition of a lady her age. Her violet eyes may have had less brilliance and sparkle than her younger days, but they were magnificent. From Grandmother's gestures and facial expression, she was merely an older version of my princess, and I knew I would be equally enamored.

Why the party was called a slumber party boggled the mind. Not one of the young ladies slumbered. They shared intimate details about attractions to certain boys at school. My Miss Devon seemed still fawn-like in the discussion of boys, which pleased me. I'd say a few were too enthused by the male gender for their age. I knew the kind and knew eventually, their friendships with Devon would wane. I couldn't imagine my girl quite so forward. The young man to win her affection would surely be made to toe the line.

As it was the wee hours, they began telling ghost stories. All the ghouls they spoke of were descriptively far-fetched. Miss Devon spoke up, saying she doubted if there were ghosts in the first place, and if there were, they would be kind and somewhat sad. If they were to be a fact, she supposed it was probably because they were caught between the living and the dead, but definitely not mean or scary. Without knowing it, she pegged the situation with accuracy. There were details only my Creator and I knew, which landed me forever bound to this house.

While I knew Miss Devon enjoyed having her friends celebrate with her, I could also tell she was more excited about time with Grandmother. I'd catch her longing smile and glance toward a clock waiting for time to pass. It was delightful when the last guest bid farewell. Quiet returned to the Hurstall home.

Grandmother had a close relationship with Miss Devon. They were similar beyond measure. She slept in Devon's bedchamber instead of one of the guest chambers, and the two would whisper and giggle beneath the cotton quilts. When Grandmother unpinned her hair, it tumbled down to the middle of her back.

Devon grabbed a hairbrush. "Please let me brush your hair. It's beautiful. Why don't you wear it loose?" She stroked Grandmother's hair as they watched one another in the looking glass. The moment was tender and filled with love.

"It wouldn't be proper for a lady my age," the sides of her mouth turned up, similar to the smile of my treasure. She held one of Devon's hands. "When I was your age, I wore my hair down like you. I'll have to send you a photo from my younger years. I think you'll find our likeness startling. I know I do." As did I.

"Grandmother, I say wear your hair any old way you want. Who cares what people say? They would only be jealous of you if they were to be so bold as to say anything at all." They smiled through the looking glass. They had a unique closeness, and it was lovely.

"My darling, you are still young; one day, you too will wear your hair differently. Is it getting any easier being here, sweetheart? Do you yearn for home as much? In many a conversation with your father, he told me of your sadness. I think he questioned the wisdom in moving from Chelsea, but I assured him, for his advancement, it had been a wise move."

"It's getting better, but England will always be home. The school is nice, and the requirements are fairly easy. My marks are the highest in the class. I actually tutor a couple of girls. Oh, but I miss you, Grandmother. I miss our lovely outings. Mother and I rarely go on an outing, and when we do, all I hear is, 'your posture is slouched, dear, or Devon, don't giggle so. It gives you a simpleton appearance. Don't Devon, no Devon, stop Devon.' We share very little in common, and it is quite sad. She and Father don't speak often, and when they do, the room fills with ice crystals. My friend's parents are much different—they hold hands, flirt with each other, and it is obvious even to me how much in love they are, but not Mother and Father."

Miss Devon was quite right. Mother and Father did not give the appearance of sharing any love, even behind closed doors. Not being a prying soul, I stayed far from their conversations, but even mere glances in their little interaction felt stale, even void of emotion.

Grandmother and Miss Devon spent much time out of the house—shopping and dining like two young girls. At home, they played cards and chatted endlessly about school activities. Laura rarely joined in, which saddened me. It looked like she longed to be one of the girls, but something inside prevented her. Sad really. Laura was far too young to have given up on happiness. The time came for Grandmother to return to England; I would miss her and her enchanting stories of travel and conquest. My young princess had a good cry and began to plan her escape to England. I knew the plans were fruitless, but if it eased her aching heart, then I would endlessly listen.

Dear Diary

Seasons came and went, and by the age of seventeen, Jeffrey would have given most anything for a mere speck of attention from the beautiful Miss Devon Hurstall.

Her bedchamber door flew open. Someone must have said or done something to aggravate my feisty young friend. Devon still resorted to scattering everything within reach whence in a temper outbreak. She threw herself on her bed sobbing. My heart broke as it did every time her feelings had been hurt. She no longer confided in Charlotte but would make entries in her diary. I felt guilty for reading as she poured her feelings through the pen onto the paper.

Miss Devon had developed into a breathtakingly gorgeous creature. She was, I would say, tall for a young lady her age. Only an inch shy of Mother, she majestically stood about five feet eight inches and had the body of a grown woman. I felt myself drawn to the rafters when she would undress or bathe. This day she remained fully clothed in her school uniform, only kicking off her shoes before flopping onto the bed. She began her entry:

Dear Diary,

Today has been one of the most embarrassing and anger-provoking days of my life. Waiting to board the school bus home, I had finished speaking with Claire when Jeffrey Charles ran in front of me, kissed me on the lips, and ran off. He is such a cowardly creep. I didn't have a chance to slap him. Claire yelled at him, but the rest of the kids just laughed. Many of the girls may think he's heaven-sent, but I maintain my disdain for him. I might have found it flattering if it had been anyone but Jeffrey Charles. As it is, he has more self-confidence than is rightfully deserved. He acts like he's God's gift to girls, and he's not. Tomorrow I shall put him in his place in front of everyone. Dirty scoundrel. All for now."

My dear Miss Devon had a determination beyond the better part of reason. She stood in front of her looking glass, admiring her attributes. I stood behind her, watching as she pivoted and turned from side to side. Her hand nearly came in contact with me; I felt a shiver run through my essence. What was this? How inappropriate of a feeling. Immediately I felt shame and guilt. I resorted to rapidly ascending to the rafters and dusty old trunks.

I sat in the wicker seat of an old straight-back chair positioned at a relic of a secretary desk Father had cloaked in a sheet. Peeking under the sheet, I found a box of nondescript stationery. I selected a slender pen, which continued to amaze me with how it might work without an inkwell at my disposal, but there seemed to be perpetual ink.

I began:

My Darling Miss Devon,

I have admired you from afar for some time now. My heart remains somber in your despair. I long to make you smile, bearing your beautifully expressive dimples. Thoughts of holding you in these struggling times puts my soul to rest—something that has eluded me for an eternity. I pray you find your happiness.
Dearly Devoted,
Sebastian

Before I begged off in fear, I quickly addressed an envelope and dampened the flap as the use of sealing wax was a thing of the past. Without pause, I went to the entrance foyer, slid the letter in, and shuffled it among the day's mail. Retreating to the attic, I began pacing, arguing the appropriateness of my actions. Finally admitting my poor decision, I slipped downstairs. Struck in disbelief, I watched as Mother perused the mail. What had I done? In a fleeting moment of absurdity, I had surrendered my heart in an idle pursuit.

Mother curiously inspected the envelope, daintily passing her thumb over the absent postage mark. I could tell she was contemplating opening the letter. She'd have no idea who the mystery Sebastian was, nor would she lose sleep over the letter. Mother seemed to be growing more distant by the day.

She set the envelope on the entry hall table, glancing back at it as she walked away.

Still cloistered in her room, Devon examined her perfect face in a handheld-looking glass. All remnants of emotion were erased. She trotted down the stairs into the kitchen where Nell, the keeper of house Hurstall, had baked butter cookies topped with a light sprinkling of sugar.

"Nellie, what smells so divine? Like a naughty temptress, the aroma captured my curiosity."

Nell held the filled platter behind her back. "Just for you!" She proudly presented the tray of treats.

"You know I can't refuse your divine biscuits. I mean cookies. Why do the Americans insist on making up their own words? Clearly, these are delicious biscuits perfect for an afternoon tea or anytime for that matter." She sat at the breakfast table, slowly picking off sugary pieces and popping them in her mouth, enjoying every morsel.

"Don't ruin your meal, Devon." Mother minded as she entered the kitchen. "Oh, but they do tantalize."

"Do have one, Mum. They're delightful. Here sit by me. We haven't visited much lately."

Mother joined Devon at the table. "My precious girl, you get more beautiful with each day. Do tell me how things are going at school. Your marks?" Mother tasted the cookie. "These are delicious! One will be my limit, and perhaps one after dinner tonight. Don't want to be a porky." Mother patted her girlish waist. Ladies could be interesting creatures. Had I been able, I would have sat and eaten the entire platter, but alas.

"Mum, my marks are all exceptional; however, there is this boy—" she paused, her eyes widened, and her cheeks became even rosier. Oh my, it was evident Devon fancied a lad at school. I must admit I was a little jealous of the young man. To have Miss Devon's affection would truly be an honor. Thus far, no one had even turned her head, and I would have known as I spied over her diary entries where she bore her soul. Nosy cad that I was.

"Yes?" Mother's eyebrows raised.

"His name is William, but everyone calls him Wills. He's on the basketball team, and when he smiles, he has only one dimple, which I think is smashing. I think he might like me. He always smiles at me when I look in his direction. What should I do? I want to talk to him, but what would I say?"

Mother smiled. " I knew this day would come, and I am truly surprised it didn't happen earlier. It is always good to let the boy make the first move. You don't want to appear easy."

My darling Devon curiously cocked her head, "I'm not certain I understand. You're saying if I talk first, he'll think I'm slutty?"

Mother put her hand to her mouth, aghast. "What a common word. Please don't speak in such a manner."

Poor Mother was caught in a time when proper protocol took a turn. She was not up with the times. Our delightful young lady had not given up even a kiss, which in these times may have been near miraculous. No, Mother, Devon was a good girl, and whether I liked it or not, she most definitely could speak to the lad. There was not as much as a hint of impropriety in the girl. I knew all her deep secrets, having intruded over her shoulder as she bled her heart.

"Very well, then maybe I'll just give him a wave, or would that, too, be whorish?" She had pushed Laura too far.

"Devon, why must you be so impudent?" Mother stood, but my girl giggled, pulling her arm and encouraging her to sit.

"Mum, you are the easy one! Easy to rattle. I knew I could get you with whorish. Relax, it's just us in this conversation, and if we can't carry on together, then that would be a sad state of affairs, would it not?"

"I suppose you have a point, but do not make common expressions part of your daily vocabulary. You do get me riled up so much my heart flutters."

"Sorry, Mum. I shall restrain myself in the future." While Devon smiled at Laura, there was a longing sadness to her countenance. Only I knew the heartbreak she held close. My poor darling was lonely for a friend. She had many acquaintances in her class, but she did not trust anyone enough to truly be friends. Claire, a classmate, enjoyed sleeping at the Hurstall home, but it was always Claire talking about herself. In my opinion, she thought a little too highly of herself, but at least it was company, and Devon did get along well with her. The girl touted being best friends with Devon, and I supposed she was the closest thing to it. I, however, knew her better than anyone due to my unnatural obsession.

"Devon dear, I almost forgot; you have a letter. The stamp must have fallen off, and I did not see a return address. Nonetheless, it is on the foyer table."

With a look of wonder, she made her way to the table. Before opening the envelope, she gave it a thorough inspection. "I don't recognize the penmanship. This is most curious." Clasping the unopened envelope, she retreated to her bedchamber. I could hardly bear this drawn-out affair. Had it been me, the curiosity would have driven me to tear the envelope open. Patience had never been one of my gifts, and as a result, I was in an eternal predicament.

She reclined on her bed with a stash of pillows supporting her back. Finally, she opened the envelope and read it.

My Darling Miss Devon,

I have admired you from afar for some time now. My heart remains somber in your despair. I long to make you smile, bearing your beautifully expressive dimples. Thoughts of holding you in these struggling times puts my soul to rest—something that has eluded me for an eternity. I pray you find your happiness.

Dearly Devoted,

Sebastian

"Sebastian. Do I know a Sebastian?" She re-read the letter several times. "Hmm, I'll have to be on the lookout for a boy watching me. He certainly seems to be extremely observant. Interesting." Her luscious mouth produced the best smile I had witnessed since she and the stuffed bear, Charlotte, pulled naughty capers. She enjoyed my letter, and it brought a smile to her face. What more could I want? An outstanding thought indeed, even if I thought so myself. I escaped to the rafters, took my seat on the wicker high back, withdrew another piece of stationery and envelope. I began:

My Darling Miss Devon,

Your perky disposition thrills my essence to the very core. How I wish we could be companions. I would endlessly listen to your thoughts of the day, your experiences with friends, and any sort of thing you held close to your heart. It pleases me greatly to have brought a smile to your face; however, I sadly regret the lack of intimate conversation between you and your mother. Both of you have a countenance of longing.

If only you and I could meet, perhaps I could be of benefit. You have too much beauty and awareness to ever be longing. Although it makes me green with envy, if you want William's attention, speak to the boy. Your mother is stuck in the rules of the past. No matter the fate of your admiration for William, I am smitten for eternity.

It sorrows me to see you unhappy and disquieted. Maybe one day we will engage, but until then,

Dearly devoted,

Sebastian

Signed, sealed, and ready, I held it until postal delivery the following day.

First Stroll

The day dragged into evening. The Hurstall family was ever so proper, unbearably so. Father occasionally would address Miss Devon. Looking at her face, I could tell she wanted more than a weatherly conversation. Mother hardly looked up from her place setting. I couldn't help but notice Mother was eating less and less. She already had a slim figure; if not careful, she might slip away to nothing. I was perplexed, I must admit. Mother and Father rarely spoke whence alone together. A peck of a kiss was even a rarer occurrence. Did Mother miss home as much as Miss Devon, even though it had been over eight years? Father was always ensconced in the financials. Neither of them was happy. The routine of their lives even bored me. Here I was locked forever to wander the house where I had been unforgivably improper. Thus my circumstance for eternity. Why the couple seemed to live a lifeless, loveless existence was unfathomable. Too soon, it would be the only way. What joy they would have missed, but it would be too late.

Sweet, full of life, Miss Devon was being dragged into her parents' nothingness. I couldn't have such a thing happen. She was a person of full character, and if they wouldn't stoke the fire, I would find a way.

She drifted to sleep holding my letter. Her sleep was disturbed by nightmares. I watched as she tossed, turned, and murmured, almost in torment. Even though I was most unpracticed at dream walking, I knew what to do. Upon discovering the ability I possessed, I had invaded the secret place of several residents. It was mere tomfoolery on my part. Dare I?

If I could quiet her fear, then I must. It was the gentlemanly thing to do. I slipped into her dream with trepidation. Suddenly I felt a tug on the leg of my trousers. Miss Devon might have been eight years of age in her dream. "Where did you come from, sir, and why are you here? Will you be traveling with me? I must warn you the monster is going to try to trick me; he always does. This time Charlotte will gain his attention while I run to the boat. We must move quickly, though. Do you want to journey with me?"

"I would be honored to journey with you, Miss Devon."

She looked oddly at me. "How do you know my name? Never mind, we don't have time to chat. Prepare yourself; when the monster appears, Charlotte will lure him in a chase. Get ready!"

Charlotte was walking next to Devon in the dream world as though she was alive. The stuffed toy looked at me and smiled. "Sir, would you kindly escort her to the destination?"

I nodded with a look of promise and honor. Of course, I would.

We came to the corner of the building. As promised, the beast jumped out, reaching for Devon. Charlotte taunted the beast. I picked up my little princess and ran with all my might as she shouted directions. I saw the entrance gate to the ocean voyager. I forced long strides past the gate master as she and I boarded. The very moment before my foot touched the deck Miss Devon awoke with a start. "Oh my!" She clutched her night dress and looked around her dark chambers. She jumped out of bed and grabbed her tattered and worn friend. "Charlotte, did you see the traveler? He carried me to the ocean liner. I made it. I'm going to be going home, at least in my dreams. " I had successfully triumphed and could bask in her joy as she giggled and hugged her stuffed bear. Her tear-filled laughter lifted my soul. I, too, wanted tears of joy. She turned on her bedside lamp, grabbed her diary, and commenced writing fast and furiously.

Oh, Dear Diary,

The most remarkable experience has just happened. I was having the same sad dream of trying to go home. Unlike usual, where the monster drags me kicking and screaming back to Mother and Father with my efforts thwarted, something strange happened. A kindly gentleman wandered into my dream. He was a nice man with light brown skin and golden eyes. I warned him about the monster, but he wasn't the least bit afraid. Charlotte asked him to get me to safety. He promised, and I trusted him. Even though he was a stranger, I wasn't fearful; in fact, I felt excited. He ran as though loping with abnormally long strides. We made it past the ticket steward, but the moment before his toes felt the deck of the ship, I woke with a start. I hope I see him in other dreams. He looked like someone I would enjoy having as a friend, even though it was only a dream. Mysterious. I hope he visits me again. Good night diary; dawn is but a few hours away.

Bless her heart. I felt alive again. Holding my precious princess awakened my heart and soul. Her words stirred inside me. While walking a tightrope between honesty and deceit, I looked forward to another dreamworld encounter.

The morning brought a disturbingly sad event. Miss Devon had already left for school, and Father was well on his way to work. Mother hurriedly packed her trunk with all of her belongings. She sat on the closed chest, fastening the latches amidst sobbing. She managed to get the trunk down the stairs, twice nearly misstepping to her certain death. I was all too familiar with the life-taking treachery of the stairwell.

Mother was clearly leaving us. I wished she wouldn't, but she was in such despair. She looked at the grandfather clock in the lounge as though rushed and quickly withdrew a card from her pocketbook. Sobbing in the lounge, she sat in one of the wing-back chairs, placed a large picture book on her lap, and began to pen her note.

My Dearest Ian,

I am certain you might find this alarming, but perhaps I give myself too much credit, and it won't matter at all. I'm returning home to Chelsea. I know those long hours that have kept you working until late hours were excuses to meet with another woman. I feel no anger toward you. Yet I know not why. There is certainly due course and an expected outcome should I feel angry, betrayed, or hurt. More so, I feel sad that we didn't at least talk as friends. Your happiness has always been a top priority; perhaps I wasn't demonstrative enough.

The passion has long been absent from our marriage, and I wish you only the best. I don't want to disturb Devon's academics, but I hope you can see to her spending summer break in Chelsea.

A knock sounded on the door. Mother answered. Standing at the door was a young man, obviously her transport. "If you would be so kind, please place my trunk in the vehicle along with these other two bags. I will be out directly. Thank you."

She held one of her laced trimmed handkerchiefs to her nose and returned to her letter to conclude.

Please do not phone nor write as this has been most difficult for me. There aren't any explanations needed. Wishing you all the best. I will contact you closer to the summer.

Laura

Sealing the letter inside an envelope addressed to Ian, she placed it on his chair, picked up her pocketbook, and left—never once looking back.

Although rarely moved with emotion, I must admit my heart felt broken. I would miss Mother but had watched as she wasted away in loneliness. I sincerely hoped she could find her new place in the world.

My thoughts instantly went to Miss Devon. What would her response be? Would Father be honest with her? While I didn't have firsthand facts, I could see the longing of his heart for another.

Laura had a lovely look to her but was weighted down by the lack of his love. I wondered if this new acquisition would cross our threshold. He dare not bed her under the beam of his daughter. All I could do was wait for my precious delight to return from school. Indeed she would pen her diary with a broken heart, and then I would know precisely where my treasure's feelings landed. I hoped it was not too much for her to bear.

What dreams might she have with this new development? I thought she very well may need my comfort and counsel, rationalizing my absurd obsession and the lengths I would go to satiate my unrequited love.

I busied myself prying into Father's belongings. Finally, I found what I imagined I would come across; certainly, Mother had found similar. Across the shoulder of one of his suit jackets was a long, distinctly blonde strand of hair. Had there been other stray hairs or even other past indiscretions? I couldn't decide which would be worse and where my thoughts on the topic fell—was it easy one-night jaunts with trollops for the fulfillment of physical needs, or had he helplessly fallen in love, through no fault, just mere circumstance? For some odd reason, I always felt an emotional betrayal was worse than sheer lust—I was experienced in both, to my grave misfortune.

Mother

The day whisked by as Nell tended to the daily chores of the Hurstall residence. Whilst dusting the lounge, I noticed as she stood staring at the envelope on Father's chair. She quickly turned and ran, as though her life depended on it, up the stairs and into their bedroom and Mother's barren closet. To my surprise, she wailed great prolonged sobs. Yes, I was saddened and maybe heartbroken, but I was around all the time, basically part of the house, as a manner of speaking. This response was unexpected, and I couldn't comprehend its impact on Nell.

From all accounts, she had not been close with Mother. They had not exchanged emotional heart-to-hearts. Being the eyes of everything in the Hurstall home, I would surely have twigged onto such closeness. Nell kept the home spotless, cooked meals, and organized the deliveries or repairs of the residence, as was her job. She gathered her wits, stuffed a tissue in her pocket, and proceeded with household chores. There were many slight sniffles throughout the day, and she seemed to get more fortified the closer the hands of the clock marched to four o'clock. *Well done,* I thought. Yes, she would need to be strong for Miss Devon and perhaps even Father, but the latter came with hesitant unlikely ponderance.

I heard the click of the front door latch and desperately needed to see her face. She seemed excited, "Mum, Mum?" She circled into the kitchen. "Nellie, where's my mother? Yum," she peered into the soup kettle. "I'm sorry, where is she?"

"Well, I'm not certain, Devon. I haven't seen her all day." I could see she was balling her fist around the tissue in her pocket. Good girl, no tears now, Nell. Not the time or the place.

"Odd." Devon sat at the kitchen table with a cluster of grapes. "Two brilliant things happened today. You mustn't tell Mum," as she plucked a few grapes and popped them in her mouth. It appeared she was sizing up Nell's ability to keep a promise. "Firstly, when the morning bell rang, Jeffrey Charles was huddled by the book lockers with some of his friends. I pushed my way through the group and slapped him square across the cheek and told him never to lay his foul lips on mine ever again, or I would report him to the front office, whereby he would be put on suspension or even expelled. I then turned and walked off with my head held high. The other boys found it most amusing, while Jeffrey Charles turned a bright red with embarrassment. Now he knows what it feels like to be humiliated in front of friends. The totally insane thing happened at lunch."

She popped a few more grapes in her mouth. "Despite Mum telling me not to talk to Wills," her eyes opened wide as saucers, and her smile was brighter than the stars above, "We spoke at lunch. It will not be a lie; I did not speak first. As I approached him, we both said hi at the same time. So effectively, I did not provoke the conversation or speak first. But here's the best bit. He asked me to meet him at the movies Friday night. Do you think they will let me go? I have to tell him tomorrow. Oh gosh, I hope they let me go! Tell me it wasn't a perfectly glorious day. Shh, no word to Mum. I want to tell her." She relaxed back in the chair with a complete look of contentment.

Then it crossed my mind. Who would be at the theater to chaperone this young man Wills and my precious Miss Devon? What if the young man tried to be too forward? I shook those thoughts from my mind as there wasn't a thing I could do. If he were here at the house, I could oversee all interactions. Seventeen, and she hadn't even had her first kiss; I was beginning to sound like Mother. The girl deserved a life, and if it involved a kiss or two, it was all a part of living. I told myself a most convincing story, but there was a touch of envy there, I must admit.

"Sounds like you had yourself a day of it. Slapped one boy and flirted with another. You sound fond of this Will." She smiled over her shoulder at the girl. I could tell she remembered the days when she was a girl and had her first love. The fairer sex tended to get a peaceful look on their face when speaking of young men. Young men were different in all aspects. Having been one, my testimony was true and accurate.

"It's Wills with an "s" at the end. He's handsome and has the best smile ever. He's several inches taller than me and nothing like the other boys; he's not a pig. When Mum comes in, tell her I'm in my room doing studies. Remember, not a peep."

"No fear of that, missy." Nell kept her back to Devon; I could see a tear balancing between trickling down her cheek or remaining on the lid, waiting to dry. She quickly patted the evidence away.

No fear indeed, I thought. I arrived just in time to see my young lass twirl around the room chanting Wills, Wills, Wills. Oh, to be the recipient of such adoration from Miss Devon! Rather than tossing her shoes on the floor, she took them off and stored them in her closet. She began to undress, which was my signal to move on for a few minutes, then I fully realized I had not put my latest note in the stack of delivered mail—a perfect time to exit and tend to my task.

After a few moments, given enough time to redress, I spied in the room. She was propped on her bed, pen in hand, about to open her diary when she was interrupted by I know not. Quickly exiting the room, she ran down the stairs, rifled through the mail, and came to a complete stop when she saw my letter. Her smile was telltale. I had won favor again even though she had not even read one word. What if I had forgotten? Would she have been sad or disappointed? No more time to spend on something that was not true; I had already wasted a lifetime thinking about alternate endings to certain situations that I would never be able to resolve.

Back on the bed, I could see her deliberating between diary and letter. Which to tend to first? I could hear myself saying, pick me; pick my letter. I sounded like a little girl. All manliness seemed to have vanished over the years; how peculiar. She slowly tore the letter open and glanced at my name.

"Sebastian, Sebastian, where for art thou, Sebastian?" She spoke in true Juliet style. She anxiously read my short letter and, with a laugh, commented, "Whoever you are, my Sebastian, and wherever you are, thank you for your devotion. I wonder why he hasn't introduced himself. Perhaps he is too shy. Curious how he knows my thoughts about Mother, about what we said regarding Wills? Hmm." She put the letter down and went downstairs to the kitchen. She stared at Nell.

"Can I help you, Devon?" Nell turned from the stove to face her.

"Do you have a son, Nellie? And do you talk to anybody about what we do or say in the house?" Devon almost looked menacing and accusatory.

Taken aback, Nell sputtered. "N-no, I have no children, and my loyalty is to you and your family. I would never break your trust. Why would you ask such a question?" Nell was obviously insulted and looked hurt.

Devon's shoulders dropped; she smiled and gave Nell a hug. "I didn't think so, but I'll let you in on another secret, one not to be shared with Mum. No, just come see." She grabbed Nell's hand and brought her to her bedchamber. Devon showed her the letters I had written. "See why I might have thought what I did. It's like this person is here with us and knows my every thought. What do you think?"

"He has beautiful lettering, almost like old-style from way back in time. Have you told any of your friends about your feelings?" Nell stood and thought for a moment. "I don't know, Devon. Pay attention when you are out and about. I see clearly why you asked me; I would have asked me too. It is strange, I agree. Maybe you should—" she stopped mid-sentence. Her mother was no longer going to be there to tell. The old girl almost tripped herself into revealing Mother's departure. I was glad she stopped in time.

"Thanks, Nellie. If I hurt your feelings by asking, I'm sorry." Devon reached down and gave her another hug.

"Missy, my skin is thicker than that. No indeed. I'm fine. When you meet this Sebastian let me know." She left the room to go back to the stove.

Devon read the letter again, sat on her bed, and opened her diary.

Dear Diary

Today has been an exceptional day. I slapped Jeffrey Charles. The jerk deserved to feel as embarrassed as he made me feel. It gives me goosebumps just to write… Wills asked me to meet him at the movies. I could just scream. I hope we see something funny and not scary. I wonder if he'll put his arm around me in the theatre or maybe hold my hand. How lovely it would be if he wanted to kiss me. I'd kiss him back, no doubt. While all the Wills stuff is exciting, nothing compares to the thrill of the mystery letter. There was another in the mail today. I wonder who it could be. Who is Sebastian? Just holding the letter sends tingles through my body. Who uses words like devoted, countenance, smitten, or longing. He sounds sophisticated. While Wills is cute and temptation on two legs, Sebastian is the throb in my heart. It is his lips I really want to kiss. I don't even know what he looks like, but he seems deep and intelligent, which I find ooh-la-la. Enough for now. To be continued… will there be another letter tomorrow and the day after? Patiently I will wait.

Oh my, with each word, I could feel, yes feel, a fluttering in my essence. The excitement was beyond anything I had experienced in over a century. How could it be?

Upon discovering my permanent situation, in the very beginning, I must admit there was sadness and hostility within me. The owners at the time would say they felt a heaviness on the landing overlooking the downstairs hall, but over the years, it vanished like time. I went through a brief episode of turning lights on to off, shutting doors, and moving things such as spectacles and the like. I guess one could postulate I matured. How desperately inappropriate and impossible, a fact I would have to deal with throughout eternity.

I had more urgent tasks at hand rather than planting myself in remorse or anger. Father would be coming home soon, and I would have to be near Devon when he delivered the sad news regarding Mother's departure.

Nell had dinner plated, waiting for Father's arrival. He liked a prompt dinner, even though his dinner hour had changed recently from six to seven, and then some nights, he did not come in until the house had been locked down and all asleep. His cold, covered plate sat waiting. Some mornings it would still be untouched and suitable only for the trash bin. Father used to be punctual and expected everyone else to be as well as they should be.

Spot on five-forty-five, he came through the door. Nell met him at the door, took his briefcase and anything else he might have on his person, such as a jacket, umbrella, scarf, and the like. "Good Evening, Nell. Can you let my wife know I'm home?"

"I'm afraid I can't, sir. I haven't seen her all day." She looked to the ground.

"All day? What on earth could she be doing all day? It's past five-thirty. Never mind. Devon? Please let her know I'll be waiting for her in the lounge, and if I could ask you to be so kind as to fix me a brandy. I believe I'll have one before dinner tonight." He moved past her and went into the lounge. It took him a moment or two before spotting the envelope.

I knew the look, and it was not good. Father's eyes squared off, and his jaw set tight. He took a seat and began to read the letter. At most, he scanned it and tossed it to the floor just as Devon walked in. "Hello, Father. I hope you had a good day at work."

"Devon, please sit." He stared at her like he was looking through her for an answer.

She sat. "Sir?" It was an awkward silent moment, and the room was thick with tension.

"Are you aware your mother has gone back to England?" His tone was most unpleasant.

Her lips parted from the shock of being blindsided. Confusion read like a sign on her face. She blinked a few times with a look of not knowing what to say, think or do. "No, Father. I don't understand. Is something wrong back home? Oh God, did someone die?" Her bottom lip began to quiver.

"No, no, Devon. Nothing like that, dear. Frankly, there's no other way to say it other than Mother has left us. More precisely, me. She didn't want to interfere with your schooling. She loves you very much. It has nothing to do with you." He looked down at his hands, twirling his wedding band around and around. "I suppose I should have seen it coming. This is hard for me to say and please let me explain." I thought, *this is going to be good; how does one tell his child he has been unfaithful to her mother? Or is he going to try to lie and catch himself as he did with the 'Mother left us,' correcting it to the accurate statement that she left him?*

"I have not been a good husband. I basically left your Mother on her own to learn the ways of living in America while my world didn't change much. Same thing day after day, you know, go to work and come home. Just a different building and a different house." *And sir*, I thought, *what about the blonde?*

"I developed a life outside of home." He raised his voice. "Nell, make the brandy a scotch." They heard her say she was on her way with it. He waited until she brought the drink; he drank half in a big gulp. He cleared his throat, circling the rim of his glass with his finger. Then with a determined look, he spoke concisely, obviously no room for discussion, "I have had a few indiscretions over the past couple of years." Oh, sir, this is your daughter; she is just like your mother. Do you really think she is going to sit quietly? You, of all people, should know better.

She was outraged. "You mean affairs? You cheated on Mum? If that is what you are saying, I don't blame her for leaving. That is disrespectful. You played her for a fool. If you didn't want to be married, I would have understood. It's obvious you and Mum haven't been happy with one

29

another for a long time, but you part ways first. She must feel terribly betrayed. Shame on you." She stood to leave.

"Wait, Devon." He almost had a plea in his voice, almost.

"Oh, don't try to explain your way out of this. There is no explanation for such behavior."

"Devon, you will adjust your tone with me. I am your father." He banged his fist on the arm of the chair.

With a quick turn on her heel, she spoke with a slaying tone, "Then act like it." And up the stairs she went. By the time she made it to her room, the tears were flowing down her lovely cheeks, cascading to her blouse, dampening the collar. She checked the time on the wall clock across from her bed. Defeatedly, she commented, "It is past midnight in Chelsea; too late to call Grandmother." She kicked off her shoes, clutched her diary in one hand, Charlotte in the other, and bent her knees to form a suitable writing angle. Silently she sat staring at the blank page. She sat the stuffed bear upon her knees and looked into her glossy button eyes. "Sometimes, Charlotte, I know I am too old to pretend, but nevertheless, I do wish you would talk to me like you do in my dreams." Her shoulders rhythmically hitched with her sobs. I could hardly stand watching this moment as my sassy young friend collapsed into a frightened, sad little girl. Her world, in one fell swoop, had changed. Mother was gone, and Father was a betrayer in the worst kind of way. She moved the bear from her knees, picked up her pen, and began:

Dearest of diaries,

My world is upside down. I am both angry and sad at the same time with both Mum and Father. While I certainly do not approve of Father's actions, I do, in some fashion, understand, maybe. Had Mum been even somewhat affectionate with him, perhaps he would not have strayed. I am not in any way excusing him, but I know the feeling of longing for her affection like I see with my friends and their mums. No mistake, what he did was beyond unforgivable, and I do not blame Mother for leaving, but it all could have been prevented if she were livelier. She seems almost dead sometimes. Her eyes always cast downward."

Her sobs grew as she wrote, rendering her helpless with the pen. It tumbled from her limp hand as she turned on her stomach, hugged Charlotte, and belted wails of anguish. Oh no, my princess, this too would pass. I sat beside her, going through the motions, tenderly petting her back.

In an instant, she stopped crying and bolted straight up in the bed, reaching for her back. She jumped to the looking glass. "What is on my back? Something crawled on me. Oh, what on earth?" She tore off her blouse at record speed. I tried to avert my eyes, but I couldn't help admiring her perfection. I tried to turn my head away but failed miserably. Admittedly, given the situation, I desired her in a most unnatural way. Convincing herself it was nothing, she calmed down and returned to her bed far more controlled. Still, in brassiere and uniform skirt, she picked up the pen. In a blink, it dawned on me; she felt my touch. Had she known it was a loving moment, not a hideous spider or other crawling creature? Perhaps she would have welcomed the sense of console. She quickly penned the word "later" and closed her diary. Before any further disrobing, I went to the rafters.

I took my seat in the high-backed chair and began to pen a note of my own.

My Darling Miss Devon,

What a devastation you endured today. My very essence felt the pain to my core. If able, I would hold you until all your fears were gone. You must forgive Mother and know it was not you she ran from. I could tell she felt alone and isolated from the world. Some of it is hers to own, some not. I am afraid, and it is my hope she will find happiness and purpose back home. My concern is you, my dearest Devon. I am truly sorry you were startled by my poor attempt to console you. It will not happen again unless invited. Please know I am forever devoted to you.

From the essence of my being,

Sebastian

There was no doubt this confession would raise suspicion, and her cleverness would put the pieces together, and my secret would be out. What would happen then? I hoped she knew better than to be afraid, but if she requested I not be near her, I would have to honor the request, and then what? I have no one to blame but myself and my careless, foolish behavior. Once again, my weakness prevailed. Even after years and years of lifeless wandering the halls, a lesson had not been learned. I felt an excited compulsion to make her aware of me and my love for her. To what end?

Changing Times

There were many postulations from my young miss, quite a change from her usual boisterous self-assurance. I watched as she weighed the actions of both her parents. Walking about the room in her nightdress, she held court, where she would be both judge and jury. Finger pointed in the air, she argued, "Let's look at the facts. Father acted like a disgusting heel, but Mum was void of feeling. She loved and still loves me but is trapped in a body that won't allow a demonstration of love. Still, she was most capable of showing her anger and outrage, not forgetting total exasperation and irritation with me. These came with ease. I wonder why?" She spun around, putting her finger to her lips. She tilted her head as though she was consumed with thought. "I wonder what her parents were like when she was a child, but then again, having them die so early in her life, had she even known them? Maybe she was sad because she didn't know them well. But Auntie Julia took on the parental role, and I supposed there were other family members. I bet there wasn't much memory of them, really. Sad. At least in Chelsea, she'll have Auntie Julia."

She glanced in the looking glass watching as she spoke. Could she feel me pacing beside her? Certainly, she would have exclaimed if she felt my essence. "The confusing bit," she went on, "is both parties are wrong in similar, but different, ways. Things often get muddled when there is love involved. I wonder if Father found love with another woman or purely the need for physical affection. Curious thought."

Curious thought, indeed. Yes, my lovely was maturing, and those thoughts of romance and all the intricacies were bound to be part of her desires. After all, it was human nature, even if I did not like the thought of some lad deflowering my perfect Devon. Would Father be involved with Devon's growing up or remain the invisible parent? The man better think carefully, or my precious princess would run to the first overture of affection. This was a thought I could hardly bear. She needed to stop this theorizing and go to sleep. I wanted to walk amid her dreams again. Could I disclose myself to her as the writer of the letters of admiration? I would hardly call them love letters though I knew they had been written with love in my heart. I was utterly smitten.

My channeled thoughts must have invaded her mind because it was not long before she gave up the debate, climbed into bed, and turned off the bedside lamp.

Her door creaked open, "Devon, are you awake?"

"Yes, Father. What do you want?" She seemed callous and cold, showing no love or compassion. If I could plead with Father, I would beg him to come to her and create more of a bond. Hardships and trying times often brought people together. This could be the opportunity of a lifetime for him.

He entered her room. Even I could detect the drink in his manner. "You must hate me, Devon. I implore you to see your way to forgiving me. I know I was wrong." He made his way to the side of her bed, turned on her bedside lamp, and sat on the bed, looking down at her. Through tearful words, he begged her forgiveness.

"Father, of course, I love you. I'm angry, but I do understand, sadly. Mum and I, over the past several years, have not been close like most mums are with their daughters. I think she wishes she could've been. She lacks the human ability to display love, I think. It frankly isn't part of her makeup." She sat up and put her arms around him. "I love you, Father, and I'm sorry. I know this must be heavy on your heart. Now I think you need to get to bed as the smell of whiskey is quite strong, and I suspect your body would be safer in bed than falling to the floor. Here." She moved him out of the way, took his arm, and guided him to his bedroom. She tucked him in bed as a parent would tuck in a child for the night, with wishes of sweet dreams and a delicate kiss on his forehead.

"Devon, you're wrong; your mother loved at one time. I'm not certain what caused her to change but whatever it was laid heavily on her heart and snuffed the light from her eyes. I won't let the light leave you, my darling."

"Good night, Father."

Well done, I thought. Devon was going to give her old man another chance. If he accepted the error of his ways, he would jump at the opportunity to engage in Miss Devon's life. What would I not give? Sleep tight, Father, for tomorrow starts a whole new life for you and your daughter, and, sir, adventures await. Of that, I promise.

Quietly she moved down the hall, climbed in the bed, and with the bedside lamp still glowing, thanked God for her father. Prayer was something she had not done since she was eight, at least to my recollection. "Good night Sebastian, wherever you may be." My answer: Right here beside you, my precious treasure.

Finally, I could hear the faint whispers of breath as she slept. With both boots, I jumped into her dream. Ahead of me, I could see her walking along a slow-moving channel, a few boats motoring by with friendly waves from the passengers on board. Hand in hand, she walked at the side of a rather tall fellow, probably a few inches over six feet, about my height. I watched as he glanced at her with an ear-to-ear smile. They laughed with one another in a young flirtatious manner. Approaching with purposeful steps was Claire. She walked up to the young man and slapped him on his cheek. Devon shrieked, "You slapped the wrong one." Horrified, the young man ran off. "Come back, Wills, please come back."

In a most menacing tenor, Claire advised, "You don't want him, Devon; he's been with me all along. He's playing you for a fool." She turned and ran off in the same direction as Wills.

I quickly ran up to her. "Miss Devon, please do not fret."

She cocked her head with a look of puzzlement yet recognition. "You're the man who saved me from the monster and brought me safely to the ocean liner." She smiled softly.

"Yes, my dear. I hope all fear is gone now. I am here for you." I looked down into her beautiful violet eyes. I could feel the love emanating from mine.

"Are you—" she dreamily began to inquire. It was not the time yet for me to tell her my name. I wanted more time with her without complication or risk of being turned away. I took her hand and resumed walking with her next to the channel. Silently we walked for what seemed too long for a dream. "Who are you? I've only seen you in the one dream. How is it that I have conjured you up? This is most peculiar, I would have to say."

"You have nothing to fear with me." I bent my elbow whilst holding her hand. It felt like life. No, better than life had actually been. Tenderly I kissed her hand. The softness of her hand was delicious, and I could feel it. Oh my, I was touching her. She felt exactly as I thought she would—like fine velveteen. Tingling, like the shiver from a cold morning mist, ran through my body and what may have been a heartbeat seemed to bound in delight. Wait, no, the bounding was her heart. "Truly, Miss Devon, you have nothing to fear."

"Mystery man, I am not fearful in the slightest, and I have no reason to believe you would inflict harm upon me. In fact, sir, I rather think you fancy me. You have a familiar twinkle in your eye, suggesting an admiration of sorts. Am I correct?"

Was this glee I was feeling? I certainly had never felt gleeful, maybe as a child, but never as a man. While I had a strong attraction to her, I think my thoughts were only in the purest of nature. I remembered the smoldering passion I had felt for my Scarlet, and this sensation was entirely different.

36

With Scarlet, the fire had emanated from my loins. Yet, this giddy feeling was not fatherly or of any other relation. For once in my existence, I was dumbfounded. I had to chuckle to myself. Yes, if there were anyone able to dumbfound me, it would be sassy Miss Devon.

"In this case, I am most fond of you, and the truth is, you are enchanting. Your charms and tenacious ways amuse me, but not in the manner you seem to be alluding." I smiled at my young friend and kissed her hand again.

Curiously she watched me and listened to every word as though calculating a response. The corners of her mouth drew up into her perfect bow-like smile. A smile I had come to love. It always warmed my essence.

In her devilish voice, I knew all too well from arguments with Mother and Father or long-winded dissertations of complaint to poor Charlotte, she addressed me. "Are you telling me, sir, you haven't any desire to kiss my lips instead of my hand?"

"Ah, I see. No, Miss Devon, I am perfectly satisfied kissing the top of your hand and have no desire to kiss your lips." She pouted regarding my response.

"Then what good are you in my dream? I may have to dream you away. I figured you were the man of my dreams that would require an embrace with a kiss on my lips whenever I so desired. Right? Yes, I am absolutely correct. You haven't even properly introduced yourself. Your name could just as easily be Tom, Dick, or Harry. Harry it will be then if you do not introduce yourself. You look like a Harry."

How Devon of her. I could not help but think I did not look like a Harry in any way, shape, or form. The only Harry I had known was a jokester, maybe one would even say, a prankster. No, no, no, I am Sebastian, and I look very much like my name. Even whilst a young man, I presented an air of sophistication. I am confident it is part of what attracted Scarlet to my side. She would say, "Sebastian, you are worldly in a most intriguing way." She would bat her eyes at me and stand close enough that I could detect a hint of perfume she used to enhance her breath. Oh, I felt the eyes of disapproval from her parents. They did not care for me and were appalled their delicate flower of a daughter had fancied me. I knew they had forbidden it, but if we were, by happenstance, to be in the same place at the same time, they could not deny her speaking with me. Had they raised a ruckus over it, not that they would have even considered it given their high birth and social ways, they would have been frowned upon, maybe even outcast, by their high society circle. It was grossly inappropriate for one to reveal the primal side of one's true nature in their circle.

Like it or not, I knew I was a most desired bachelor. Enough transporting my own thoughts during this lovely setting of her dream. "Harry, how old are you? Should you even be in the dream of a young girl?"

"Miss Devon, at any point, you may dream me away, and," I snapped my fingers, "I would be gone. No, I think you feel entertained by my presence. To answer your question about my age, it is a most difficult one to answer. I'll go with twenty-one." I could see her muster a look of formidable engagement and ready to battle, oh my, but it was endearing.

"Harry, you are either twenty-one or not. How stupid to pick an age. It's a clear and concise answer, no supposition involved." What a spark of challenge; this was going to be fun.

Walking in her dream allowed me many experiences I had not felt in over a century. "But, you see, Miss Devon, in your dream, you can be seventeen one minute and the next eight or ten or even an adult. An adult might prove difficult as you have never been one. You are bright; I imagine you understand the illogical logic of your dream world."

We continued to walk. I felt a change coming. Were we going to shift in time or place? I spotted the executor responsible for the fluctuation in the atmosphere. We strolled off the pathway, making our way to a pristine forest. The trees were tall, with limbs full of evergreen leaves and birds chirping sweetly. On the edge of the forest was Mother. The closer we drew, I could see it was the mother she loved so dearly as a young child. She had the soft complexion of a young woman, perhaps in her mid-twenties.

Devon was a bit harsh at first. "Hello, Mother. This is my friend Harry.

I spotted you over here. Trying to run away and hide from me? Was that your plan? I foiled it for you as I am most observant. I am quite irritated with you." Mother went from a look of joy to sorrow.

I interjected. "Laura, you look stunning today. Having a stroll are you on this exquisite day?"

I could almost feel the daggers shot my way from Miss Devon. They would have plunged deep. My very essence felt the coldness of her look, but then as quickly as she imparted her hostility, a radiance broke through.

"Mother, I have been most angry with you, but I forgive you. Moving on, where are you going, and would you like to stroll with Harry and me?" She put on an inviting smile. Good girl.

Mother immediately perked. "Where are you going, may I ask?" How sweet Mother's expression was. There was no doubt she loved her little girl.

"We are going to board an ocean liner and return to England. I was actually going to go to our old house, figuring you may very well be there, but I see you have not made it to the boat yet. Would you like the pleasure of our company?" The pleasure of our company? How audacious of Miss Devon. One day she might discover humility and grace at some point, but it was not on the horizon from my perspective.

"No, thank you. My way is through the path in the forest. I need to see the forest."

Miles away, a voice called out to Miss Devon. I quickly exited her dream without a notice of departure. I felt rude but waking by startle from a dream jolted me, which was a most unsettling experience for my essence. "Devon, honey, you've overslept. You must get a wiggle on. I have breakfast plated and waiting for you." Was Nell going to take this little fledgling under her wing? If that indeed was her intention, the battle with Miss Devon could be cutting. I had witnessed it all too often with Mother and Father. She certainly was opinionated and felt the need to share her opinion with everyone in the house because she was always right. Even I, with my fascination for her, felt like rolling my eyes on many an occasion, which was one of her favorite moves of impudence.

As she sat up, stretching and yawning, she had a smile on her that was radiant. "Down in a sec, Nellie." She woke up as sweet Devon this morning. We should all feel blessed. I often wondered what she was like in the outside world. Was she a house devil/street angel? A pleasant thought. It was time for me to return to the rafters as she got out of bed. She began in a sing-song manner. "Hello, Harry! How are you, Harry?" She put particular emphasis on the H. Oh dear me, this was not my intention. I wanted to say to her, remember old Wills.

This was the age when young girls and lads could be ever so fickle. One moment it was Wills, then Sebastian, then Harry. I had my fair share of randy interests as a boy, but nothing came close to the love of my life, Scarlet. Thought for another time for this old soul, I supposed.

Libations

The adjustment to Mother's absence proved interesting. Miss Devon coddled Father, and he, in turn, came home earlier to greet her after school, but I watched as he befriended libation to a fault. My little lady would often navigate the way for him to his bed. With time, the sting and oddity of it all would wear off, and then we would see the proof in the pudding, so to speak. If Father did not watch himself, he would find permanency at the bottom of the bottle. Strong drink could be a masked devil preying on those with a broken spirit.

It took everything I had not to invade Miss Devon's dreams night after night. I kept it to once a week. She always seemed delighted to see me. Her eyes sparkled when she gazed into mine. I could tell she was quite smitten with my character of Harry and determined to capture romantic attention. Countless times she tried to steal a kiss. I had become a master of dodging her lips, knowing all the while she was increasingly getting frustrated as well as determined. The determination she had as an eight-year-old, while substantial and adorable, was no match for her relentless persistence as a young woman. My letters continued to be a highlight of her afternoon. She would run upstairs, quickly shut her door, and read. Her cheeks took on a soft blush as she read through my words, and she always followed her read by dreamily saying my name. It felt good for this old soul. I felt relevant, included, and for an instant, alive. On occasion, I referenced a dream or a bout of Father's inebriation. In those moments, she would stop and look around her room, perplexed by the information her secret admirer had written in the love letter.

This particular evening after school, she waited in the lounge for Father. He was a bit later than usual.

"Father, I need to speak with you. It's ever so important; please don't lollygag." She sat prim and proper, waiting for him. Her choice of words amused me to no end. Lollygag, tsk, tsk. Had a child spoken to an adult in such a manner when I was a lad, there would be consequences of the highest degree. Yes, cheeky behavior as such would have resulted in a sure switching. She tapped her foot and drummed her fingers along the arm of the wingback chair.

Glass in hand, Father entered the lounge. He had a sprawling smile. I supposed he found her comment as amusing as I did. "What is of such great importance, dear, requiring I not lollygag, you said? Do I often lollygag? Do tell." He took his seat. "Well? Be quick with it."

If eye-rolling were a competition, Miss Devon would win handsomely every time. She cleared her throat. Oh my, this was going to be something; as she pinned her shoulders back and sat high in the chair, she was ready for battle. "There are two matters I wish to address with you." Father tipped his chin with a look implying her tone needed to be tidied up. She understood and continued with a softer tone. "Wills has invited me to the school basketball game, which he will be playing in, and then to a party following the game. I will require a ride there, or I can merely stay after school and wait, which in all honesty, would not be my first choice. I would like to come home and dress more appropriately for my date." Devon awaited a response.

Father drew in a deep breath and then, with a sigh, agreed to take her to the game. "Would you have any objection to me watching the game with you?" Her eyes betrayed her thoughts regarding his suggestion. "Devon, my dear, did I say something wrong? You have a most peculiar look on your face. It's as though you smelled something foul."

Turning her head away from him, she pondered his question, then turned back. "If you must. I suppose it might do you some good to get out amongst people. There will be other parents there; however, it is usually the parents of players or cheerleaders. Nonetheless, it would make me happy if you accompanied me. There is one condition, no adult beverage before the game." I could well see her point. Rumors would fly around the school about Father if he smelled of strong drink or acted peculiar. Those kinds of things were uttered in whispers, and before long, everyone was privy. I was unsure as to her openness about Mother moving back to England. Surely, there would be a few single women whom he might intrigue. American women loved the British accent, and truthfully he was rather dapper and would make quite the catch.

"You said two questions?" He waited for the other shoe to hit the floor. "Father, do you ever get the feeling there is a presence in the house? Lately, I've noticed a fragrance. It smells more like a man's cologne than perfume." Was she talking about me, or was she speculating about him having a late-night visitor? No, I knew there had not been one late-night visitor. If Father was having a rendezvous or two, it was not in the house.

Father tilted his head to one side and put a finger to his lips to ponder the proper answer. He had learned years prior not to disregard her thoughts and deem them childlike. "No, I've never felt a presence in our home, nor have I picked up on an unusual fragrance. Are you suggesting our home may be haunted? I know many local people take ghosts and the like to heart. I, personally, have no opinion on the subject. So far in my life, I have not had the experience of meeting a departed soul." How tempting it was to start playing the old games of tomfoolery, but best I not go down that path. I felt confident I would reveal myself to Miss Devon at some point in time. I dare say she might already suspect, given her question, but did she consider the presence, as she defined it, to be the author of her daily letters? She had not mentioned it specifically in her diary nor alluded to anything of the sort in her dreams. My sly and clever girl, if she did believe someone roamed the halls of this home, she also knew if she let on in any way, the excitement and thrill might end once revealed. This was a circumstance I needed to give thought to and not let the overzealous side of my essence cloud reason.

"That was all, Father. Thank you, and I look forward to our evening together at the game." She popped up and headed out of the lounge but stopped for a quick peck on the top of Father's head.

"Don't lollygag, Devon," he snickered. "Dinnertime is rapidly approaching." His eyes glistened as he called back to her. Yes, my young friend was a most remarkable young lady, and while Father was imbibing a smidge too much, I could feel a sense of calm taking hold of him as though he had accepted the outcome of his failed marriage.

Rifling through the delivered mail, she spotted my letter and hastily ran upstairs whilst opening it. "This Sebastian has me most curious," she proclaimed to Charlotte, her old stuffed bear. "Before I even begin to read his letter, I predict he'll mention something about Father's love of hard liquor or consumption rate. He'll more than likely reference Wills or Claire, but I'm ever certain he will remark about my eyes or lips. I wish I knew where to find him. Sadly, he doesn't even know how much I adore him and his loving letters."

She kicked her shoes off and lay flat on her stomach, propping her elbows beneath her and holding the letter at eye level.

My Darling Devon,

Of late, my dear, you seem restless in your slumber. Is there perhaps anything causing you anguish or unhappiness? If only I could hold you and quiet your fears. I know Father has had a rough spell drowning his feelings in the bottom of a bottle. Do not judge him too harshly, my lovely. He needs your utmost love, care, and support in these trying times. He will come around. I do hope all is well on the Wills front. I must admit I feel slight pangs of jealousy at times and long to be the captor of your heart.

Deeply Devoted,

Sebastian

She dramatically addressed the room with a wry smile on her face as though knowing I was standing but two feet from her. "Oh, if you only knew Sir Sebastian, you have my heart above and beyond anyone else. I wish you were not as shy; then we could perhaps exchange a word or two— maybe even a kiss." She giggled. As usual, she placed my letter in her diary with all the others. It tickled me to see her read over each letter trying to put the puzzle together, although frankly, I think somewhere inside, she knew the truth. The adventure seemed in part to be the not knowing.

The closer the evening of the basketball match approached, the more her mood balanced on giddy. She tried on countless ensembles. Rather than retreating to the rafters, I merely turned my back. There had been a few occasions when I had a glimpse of her nearly naked. Her skin radiated a pale glisten or sheen like a fine pearl. It looked as though it would be like satin to the touch.

These unsettling feelings and thoughts punched hard in my gut, making me feel like one of the lecherous plantation owners that would not give a second thought to ravaging the body of a young girl. I always found it to be disgustingly grotesque. My father seemed to turn a blind eye to the debauchery. Being a merchant, increasing his profits appeared to be his only concern, and the actions of his clientele seemed invisible to him or not worthy of comment. Nothing escaped my mother's hawk-like eyes. I could read her expressions and knew exactly what she thought about some of Father's clients, but she certainly embraced the lifestyle and fineries.

The well-heeled families of color from Boston brought more sophistication and etiquette to the area. Our family was blessed with golden complexions, blue or light gold eyes, and chiseled facial features like European aristocracy. We were quite a handsome class. My sister Marcelle created a wake of turned heads as she sashayed down the street. I did not care for the enamored eyes following her moves. They were all wolves in sheep's clothing.

I am sure Miss Devon turned many a head. It was a blessing I was held to the confines of the mansion on St. Charles Avenue.

It appeared my darling had narrowed the ensemble selection to three choices. She lay them on the bed, inspecting them. "I must look sharp but fun, stylish but not trendy, and most of all, I must look alluring."

Alluring? Really Miss Devon at your young age, alluring, hmpf. She began to disrobe, and gentleman that I fancied myself to be, I turned away. Had I been watching, I could have avoided the situation. Whilst striking poses, she ran directly into my path, her arm linking into mine for only a moment, but it was enough.

She backed away at first, then with a most determined stare, she came toward me. I should have moved, but I froze. Those eyes, they knew. I had to face the music. To be truly honest, somewhere in my being was the need for her to know.

"Whoever you are, there is no doubt in my mind now whatsoever. Show yourself. How rude to spy on me. The very least you could have done was introduce yourself. Now, be quick with it." As she wished, I presented myself. Her eyes sparkled with delight. "Harry! I should have known, you scoundrel. How wonderful!" She stood right in front of me and tried to embrace me. Unfortunately, it would not be the embrace she longed for, nor I, for that matter. Our physical abilities to embrace were not possible except in her dream, where both of us were spun from thin air.

"My dearest Devon, you can sense the occasional electricity, but I am afraid we cannot embrace, my dear."

"Harry, I want to know more. I suppose I must make the most of my dreams then." She smiled with a devilishly seductive expression. Her eyes beckoned for more. "Which outfit do you like the most? Which one makes me look more alluring?" I rolled my eyes. "Excuse me? Did you roll your eyes in my direction? Swine."

"The ensemble you are wearing is quite nice. Perhaps you could fasten another button. I fear your friend Wills might get the wrong impression, dear. The imagination is far more gratifying than the reveal. Especially knowing that once revealed, it is intended solely for his eyes and not just anyone."

"Point taken." She fastened one more button cloaking the cleavage beneath. She quickly stowed the other clothing away and left the selected look draped over a chair. Sitting cross-legged on her bed drew my mind back to the eight-year-old princess that captured my heart from day one. "The game is tomorrow, and I can hardly wait." With a cocked head, she had a genuine look of ponderance. "Harry—"

"Sebastian," I corrected.

She lay back on her bed, giggling with glee. "How absolutely delightful. I love your letters. They are the thrill of my day, but then again, you already know, do you not?"

I felt a smile come across my face. "My delightful Devon, yes, I have heard your remarks, and honestly, it is the most flattering thing I could possibly hear. Every word certain as my night is long." She pulled out her diary stuffed with letters pressed between the pages. As she wrote, she read aloud.

Dear Diary,
Today has been filled with an adventure I have sought for some time. I finally know who Sebastian is, and I have exacted where the lurking—"

"Lurking, is that how you view my essence? You have struck a knife to my soul. I do not lurk; I observe, keep watch over, anything but lurk."

Her giggle was contagious, and I found myself laughing right beside her. I had longed for this interaction. Once there was an elderly man residing in the house. For some reason, I was always visible to him. He was under the illusion I was his nephew Andrew, but other than elderly Franklin, I had been void of any conversation or likeness of life. Perhaps by choice, but nonetheless, this new exchange lightened my spirit.

"Does knight in shining armor appeal more to your self-image?" She inquired.

"Devon, you are too sassy, bordering on cheeky. Do you know that?" I smiled at her.

"On occasion, I have been referred to as both sassy and cheeky, but only by those who love and adore me. How about I refer to you as my love?" I raised an eyebrow. She smiled and said, "Friends, then, and leave it there?"

"Dutifully and proudly, I shall remain your friend." She put her arm over my chest and watched as it sunk into my nothingness.

"Sebastian, I could feel tingling on the inside of my arm. What could you feel?"

I gazed into her beautiful violet eyes. "A slight shiver."

She popped up, "Oh well, I must give it a go next time I see you in my dream. I'm going down for supper, you are more than welcome to be my guest, but I guess you have sat in on many of our meals." Out the door and down the steps, she went full of rambunctious life. This one exciting episode marked the highlight of the century. What else might I have in store from my young friend? Other than the living and dead aspect of our friendship, we were well suited for one another. I was barely twenty-one when I met my demise; alas, I felt ancient compared to her young life. My eyes had witnessed over a century and a half of change, and through the years of raging controversies, perhaps I had gained insight or wisdom. Had I to do it all again, I would refrain from my poor attempt of revenge borne from anger, sadness, and hate. My poor, poor Scarlet—may her father rot in Hades for eternity.

Ah-Ha!

Much as I desired, I refrained from walking in her dreams. There had been too much to comprehend, and I certainly did not want to start something destined for failure and disappointment. Her entry in the diary remained incomplete. Would she ever complete it? I wondered what she was feeling. The night was long as I watched her slumber away. I knew from the very beginning a reveal would change the dynamics of our relationship. Should I be at her beck and call? Questions were numerous and prolific. I was in unchartered waters, and my selfish desire pulled her down the rabbit hole with me. Once again, I had cast my whims ahead of prudence and sensibility. The hundred-plus years had not made me the slightest bit wiser in matters of love. My dearest Devon was absolutely correct when she proclaimed my true desire to kiss her lips rather than her hand. Oh, why did I not realize the complexities prior to my actions? I retreated to the rafters making idle threats never to stroll the halls of my after-life home again.

The rays of the sun hailed the new day. I heard Miss Devon calling to me in a loud whisper. "Please, Sebastian, show yourself again that my day may begin with brightness. Please." I remained in the straight-back chair.

Apparently, she surmised the situation; of course, she did. "Have it your way. I thought our friendship was something I could depend upon, but I clearly was mistaken. Men, unreliable!"

I exclaimed as I swept into her room. "Men, unreliable? And Miss Devon, our friendship is one on which you may depend. I believe I made a grave mistake in presenting myself to you. The box has been opened and cannot be closed again but try, I must." I stood tall with my arms crossed in front of me, making an attempt at conviction. She walked right past me as though I was not there. Surely she could see me. Going about her tasks of readying for school, she continued to ignore me, actually humming a melody. "I refuse, Miss Devon, to entertain your frivolity and utter disregard."

With a lighthearted laugh, she turned on her heel and began, "Oh, Sebastian, you are just as easily rattled as Mother! I merely wanted to wish you a good day and tell you how sorry I was you didn't visit me in my dreams. I am certain you would have enjoyed yourself." She turned and stared me in the eye and kissed my lips, almost falling through to the floor. "Hope it was better for you than it was for me!"

I am certain I would have blushed if I had blood coursing through my body. Over the past few weeks, she had appeared different. She had always been sassy and precocious with a mind of her own, yet, now, some of her expressions sounded like a voice wiser to the way of the world. I wondered what had opened this door. Had it been the night at the movies with Wills? Perhaps. "Miss Devon! Where do you hear such things? You sound like some randy young lad. Such chatter is too common for you. Hold more poise. Tsk. Tsk."

After collecting her handbag, she turned in the doorway. "There will be no need to wallow in missing Mother; you, Sir, appear to have jumped right into her shoes! We must talk later once school lets out. Ta." She flitted down the stairs without a care in the world.

Hard as it may be to fathom the thought, was there validity to her claim of me being like Mother? Had the years and solitude stolen the once fun-loving character admired by many? Had I, in fact, transformed into an old relic without any understanding of the current times? How could I possibly advise my treasure on the ways of the world if I had lost touch? What was this 'hope it was better for you than it was for me?'

I remembered the fun I had with the advent of television—almost driving the owners mad, turning it off and on. They would get in right rows, accusing one another of the travesty of turning the device on and off without cause. Then there were the times I would sit with old Franklin and watch the broadcast. Thinking upon it, perhaps such exercises kept me relevant to popular thoughts and trends. I turned on Miss Devon's television. I was spoiled for choice. It was mesmerizing, and after an hour or two, I realized my beauty was quite tame by society's standards. The language was appalling, the nudity in abundance and sexual relations were on the box for all to see. And there it was, after sexually exploiting a man much her junior, the temptress inquired of her lover a similar question to Miss Devon's.

I warned Devon about my lack of substance. She felt it when her arm crossed my girth, sinking into nothingness. Why would she think my lips would be any different? If kiss me, she must; we could arrange the encounter during a walk in her dream.

The sound of Nell hoovering the stairs disrupted my fantasizing of scenarios whereby I may exact a kiss. With curiosity, I replayed the series of events leading to this moment. These thoughts and desires were first on display by Devon in her dream. Truth be told, I had not given thought to kissing her. My feelings for my beautiful princess transcended any male-female physicality. I had been the picture of propriety.

When she entered Devon's bedchamber, Nell's first action of business was turning off the television, then she hung the evening's attire away, oh dear. I waited until she returned to the kitchen, retrieved the clothing, and displayed them on the chair precisely as Devon had initially determined. Tempted as I was, I did not turn the television back on but retired to the attic and penned a letter.

My Darling Devon,

Where shall this new path lead? You know as well as I that we have crossed a taboo boundary. Without foolishness and with clarity, we must address this unique situation. I anticipate with delight our next exchange.

Devotedly yours,

Sebastian

Time seemed to stand still as I awaited her return from school. Where would I begin? What would she want to know? I knew how inquisitive my precious friend was and feared she might inquire about my past and how I came to this unfortunate situation. Perhaps I could direct the discussion by going straight to dream walking and avoiding any reference to the past. Given her natural curiosity, I could see where dream walking might obscure the past for a short while. I needed to remember I held the trump card. If ever I was too uncomfortable or vulnerable, I could always disappear for another century. When and why had I become such a worrisome mess? Perhaps if I had been a bit more cognizant and weighed outcomes as a young man, my situation would be much different, and I could be basking in the light of my Creator with Scarlet.

On to matters at hand. I could feel my impatience mounting and my longing for beautiful Devon growing by leaps and bounds. I took a once around her chamber, examining each trinket and adornment. I spied her photograph collection mixed in with a diverse selection of stories from historical accountings to the classics. It was interesting how similar our preferences were in literature and mystery novels.

While walking the paths of the living like most young men of my time, I had no desire to read tales of romance; I far preferred the game of pursuit and victory. Oh my, had I truly been that much of an unbridled brute? Of course, such was the situation until Scarlet, the one true love of my life. In those days, my every thought was of her with burning from my loins throughout my body, swelling with lust. One could speculate, when it came to Scarlet, I was driven by my pants and, yes, my heart rather than prudence and good measure. All caution was thrown to the wind.

Flipping through the collection of photographs told the story of my young friend's life. England appeared enchanting with lovely rolling green pasturelands. The landscapes must have been captured on a day outing. The lovely Devon was a mere babe in arms. As I flipped the pages, I watched her go from a coddled baby to a precious toddler. Even then, I could see defiance in those violet eyes. There were many photographs from her brief time at the all-girls academy. The faces she pulled for the camera were delightful and full of sass.

A rushing feeling filled the air as she returned from school. "Nellie! Nellie! Come quick."

I detected Nell was scurrying to the front of the house. In a breathy voice filled with concern, "Devon, what's wrong, dear? Are you alright?" I, too, had made my way to the front door in a blink of an eye. Oh my, she put Nell's heart on edge for a teenage girl's moment of drama.

"It is better than all right but ever so nerve-wracking. The game is tonight! I have to look my very best! Any word from Father? He must not be late, or I will be angry." She rushed for the stairs. "Oh, and please, please let me know when he arrives. And do not under any circumstances make him a cocktail. No adult beverages was our agreement."

I managed to get the photograph book put back before she entered the room.

"Sebastian, are you near?" She turned, scoping the room.

Taking form, I answered. "At your service, mademoiselle. What can I do for you?"

"I'm perplexed. My first date with Wills was when I met him and a load of his friends. Once in the dark theatre, he put his arm around my shoulder and nuzzled his face in my hair. I knew he wanted to kiss. I gave him a quick peck, and he asked me if I had ever kissed anyone before. Evidently, I didn't do it right. We will be alone in his car tonight, and I know he will want to kiss." Her vibrant violet eyes had a look of pleading.

It was clear what she was asking of me. How does one explain the art of kissing? Truth be told, back in the day, I swooned many a young lady with my kiss. Why I felt compelled to assist is a truth I needed to face and soon. It would start a slide down a slippery slope. Her plump natural pout was tempting; I certainly could not sit in judgment of the boy. "My dear, I think you need to rest for your date. A quick nap will give you a bright, refreshed feeling. Now do as you are told and not another word." I shook my head at my foolishness.

"But—"

"Shhh, Scarlet."

She gave me a most peculiar look. "Don't you mean Devon?"

"That is what I said."

The look she gave me was almost menacing. "No, sir, you said Scarlet."

I was dumbfounded, but the blunder spoke volumes. "Excuse my error, please. Off to sleep now. No time to waste."

It took about half an hour for Devon to fall into a sound sleep. Boldly I stepped in. There was nothing but darkness. I whispered her name. As though walking on an ink-black sea, she appeared. Curious, she asked, "Am I dreaming? It doesn't feel like any dream I've ever had, odd." Within seconds scenery began to appear. She and I stood face to face as she reinvented her house, zooming in on her bedroom. She started to turn, looking around her bedroom. I pulled her to me, cradling her waist in my arms. I felt her body release all her mounted tension. Carefully I swept her hair to the side. Her long graceful neck looked inviting, so I leaned down and kissed her behind the ear. It was utterly delightful, and I could feel her knees buckle ever-so-slightly. She turned in my arms; her rose-colored lips beckoned to me. I pulled her even closer, my lips a mere centimeter from hers.

Then our lips touched. It was magnificent. She succumbed, lips parting, welcoming a slight tease of my tongue. For a brief moment, her body stiffened. Reflex took over, and while I held her even closer with one hand, the other I delicately placed on the side of her face and into her lovely thick mane, letting her know all was well. She followed suit with soft wisps of her tongue, orchestrating a remarkable duet. I hated to end lesson one, but it was time. I backed off. I could feel a flush of heat in my face, perhaps as a reflective response radiating from Miss Devon.

"Sebastian, please kiss me again. I am not certain I have picked up on the finer details of kissing." She stood on her toes and, with both hands, guided my face to her. She initiated the second kiss. Flashing through my mind, I wondered exactly what I might be capable of in her dream world. What idle thoughts for this old essence of mine.

"Time to wake, my darling," I said as I pulled from her embrace. She pouted in the same delicious manner I found so adorable when she was a child. I stepped from the dream with haste. Her world of dreams felt invigorating yet harnessed a silence of dread knowing it was only fleeting at best. Her waking was like a beautiful ballet with graceful stretches upwards; her back arched perfectly to allow for a cascade of tumbling dark waves and curls nearly reaching the small of her back. To think I had a hands grip in her billowy silken hair only moments earlier.

"Sebastian, are you still here?" she cooed. "Your kiss was most divine. I suppose the true question remains; did I appear to reciprocate in a proper manner?" I chuckled to myself. How would one express the burning I had given the odd predicament of my only being an essence of a man? This was something I had not felt since that most misguided evening.

"You, my darling, not only reciprocated properly but excelled to the highest degree. Your beau should be more than satisfied, and if not, leave him by the wayside."

Miss Devon looked stunning in her casual yet sophisticated attire. The last touch was a hint of perfume and a light coat of rouge to her lips. She turned off her light and tiptoed down the staircase. In a faint whisper, she thanked me. I wanted to respond that the pleasure was all mine but stayed silent.

"Nell, is Father home? I did not hear him come in. Oh, I do hope he isn't late." She examined herself in the looking glass in the foyer.

A gentle swish announced Nell's approach as she bustled from the kitchen. As she approached, they both turned to the sound of Father descending the stairs. "Mr. Ian, you look dapper tonight."

The man had a sophisticated way about him. He always appeared well-polished and groomed to perfection. His face brightened when he saw the smile on Devon's countenance. "Father, Nell is one hundred percent correct. You look dashing and ideal for the game. You are wearing the school colors; how perfect."

There was no doubt in my mind Father purposely dressed in school support, trying to win favor with Devon. "Darling, no time to waste if we want to get a good seat. Nell, we will return late this evening. Batten down the hatches and get home early."

While it was delightful to hear the lighthearted laughter between Father and Miss Devon, the house felt empty and my soul somewhat dejected. My mind rolled back in time. I could see and hear laughter, lovely music, and New Orleans' gentry donned in their finest.

My first visit to the mansion on St. Charles was with my parents. I recall the resentment I felt being paraded to the homes of my parent's friends. Our carriage pulled up, and even as a lad, I was impressed by the beauty of the house. I abhorred the façade of gentility etched on some of the elders' faces. Whilst purveying the surroundings, my eyes fell on the vision of beauty across the room. I watched as she put her slender hand in front of her luscious lips, attempting to conceal her sweet feminine amusement. She was simply angelic. Her soft yellow curls framed a dainty face accentuated by innocent doe eyes filled with wonder. Our eyes locked for a brief moment. Albeit a mere flash, a warm rush directed its way from my heart to my stomach, landing in the deepest part of my loins. I did not think I had ever seen such beauty. I accompanied my parents as they made their way around the room, exchanging niceties. Finally, the host had a free moment. Before I knew it, the glorious creature was before me. Our eyes danced in a flirtatious manner. I could tell I was not alone in the feeling of admiration. Her face flushed when our eyes met. On the travels home, I was dismayed to hear Scarlet was already betrothed. Oh, just the mere remembrance wrenched my gut. These thoughts served no purpose other than remorse.

I made my way to the attic; perhaps penning a letter might encourage time to pass, but my anxious thoughts rendered me unable to compose anything. I felt like an expectant father pacing the floor, awaiting an announcement regarding the birth of my heir.

Hope of hopes, young Wills provided my darling Devon with an enchanted evening similar to her expectations. Young boys could be insensitive when it came to the fairer sex, and I hoped she melted his heart as she had mine. Hers was a deliciously divine kiss, and as suspected, the student mastered the skill equal to the teacher.

The clamoring of keys at the front door engaged my attention. Would she tell me of the evening or enter the experience in her diary? Nosy cad that I am. The uglier part of me wished ol' Wills came up shy, dampening her attraction to him. Alas, Father came through the door, to my disappointment. Surprisingly, he ushered an attractive blonde to the parlor.

"Cecilia, give me a moment while I pour. What is your pleasure? We have anything you could want. Perhaps a brandy? A liqueur? I make a mean Irish coffee, so I have been told." He gently smiled. My, he was charming indeed, and she was enamored, no doubt. He could have bedded her without the drink, but I hoped he would consider Devon and the awkwardness such pursuit could render.

She cooed back, "Whatever you think will be fine."

"I will be but a brief moment." He winked at her and went directly to the kitchen. He quickly threw together a plate of cheese and crackers, added a bowl of strawberries, and, passing by the beverage bar, grabbed two brandy snifters and an opened half-empty bottle. He moved with such assurance and confidence, and from the look on our guest's face, she was taken aback by his gallantry. What was it about an English accent that mesmerized the fairer sex? It was a perplexing observation I had regarding American ladies.

As she crossed her long shapely legs, she seemed to settle quite comfortably into the settee. "Ian, I could hardly believe my eyes when I saw you at the basketball game. Then, I couldn't have been more surprised to find out your daughter was the Devon I had heard so much about from Wills." She sat poised with her hand lightly touching her lips. "She is quite beautiful indeed. The last time you and I met was at the Bolivar. Do you remember?" She batted her eyes. *Hm*, I thought, *that's where the long blonde hair on his jacket came from.* While she was silver screen pretty and slathering on the femme fatale, I could not help myself thinking Mother was far more attractive if only she had smiled and lightened up. Shame on you, sir. "I was sorry to hear the two of you split ways and your wife returned to England." The look of sorrow she projected was utterly forced and transparent as the garden window. Dear, she would have done better keeping her mouth shut tightly. It was not her place to talk about Mother even if they had parted ways. I felt somewhat defensive and disgruntled.

In a flash, Father and Miss Cecilia commenced passionately kissing; the only thing coming between the two was the clothes they wore. Father had failed to lock the front door and in bounced a giggling Devon. Her eyes quickly spotted the lover's lane behavior on the lounge settee. There was shock on all faces in the house. "Father!"

"Mom?" Wills questioned. "What the hell?"

"Wills, I beg your pardon?" My lovely Devon interjected.

Outraged, the young man hurled a few insults, turned on his heel, and was back out the door with Devon following closely. Whatever she told the boy influenced him to enter once again, and the two breezed by the lounge to the kitchen. Devon whispered, "Not one more word from you about the situation. They are both single and obviously attracted to each other. For all we know, they feel the same way about our being together." Backing him up to the refrigerator, she draped her arms around his neck and drew him into a kiss. I could see the boy's knees buckle from her passion.

He pulled away. "Where has that been hiding? We need to shut this down now; your dad is in the other room."

She kissed him again, and I could see her drawing his body into hers. The poor lad was out of his league. This time she backed away, glancing slightly below his belt. Yes, my dear, that is precisely why young Wills wanted to call it a night. A conversation for another time. I truly wished Mother had addressed the birds and the bees but evidently not.

No sooner had the boy left when Devon was up in her room. I figured I would hear her call my name any moment, but all that could be heard was silence, which was deafening to me. Quietly she put her clothes away, slid into her bedgown, and turned off her sidelight. This would never do. I sat on her bed. "How was your date, darling?"

"Nice."

That was all she was prepared to share. Oh, but no, no, no. "Nice? After a week's worth of preparation for the event, I expected it to be more –"

Devon answered in an annoyed voice. "No. I cannot believe you are going to play games with me. I know you saw everything. Please do not insult my intelligence."

"Perhaps I felt the need to inquire because I had seen only part of the evening. Remember, my dear, I have no way of knowing unless it is in the house. For instance, who won the game? Did your Wills play well? Where did you go following the game? Did you have an enjoyable time? I saw the interaction between your father and Miss Cecilia. She seems to be a nice lady. I saw Wills' disapproval but saw you come back inside with him. I saw your delightful kiss and the second kiss as well. All my cards are on the proverbial table."

She sat up and turned on the bed light. "If you must know or really even care to know. Wills played well, and our school won the game. Father and I sat a few rows from Wills' mother. She tried to gain my father's attention the entire game, but he was truly interested in the game and spending time with me. I don't mind that he asked her out following the game, but bringing her to my home and acting like a dog in heat bothered me even though I told Wills not to be upset. Before long, if this continues, he will have her in my mother's bed, and I will not tolerate such behavior. Like they say, 'get a room!'"

"I see." I moved to her dressing table. "It had nothing to do with your intimate moments?" I paused. Silence. "Speak with your father alone, and before he has had a beverage, oh, and darling, leave your attitude at the door. He is sensible and will understand, of that I am certain." How could I be so brazen? I had no idea if Father would understand or if he would feel as though Devon was being impudent and speaking where she was not welcome. "Anything perplexing about the evening?"

"No. My fascination with Wills is waning." She drew the covers to her chin as she did as a child. All that was missing was the pout and Charlotte. I could see her disappointment. "His smiles no longer tickle inside or make me imagine being close to him." Throwing back the cover, she sat on the side of the bed. "Did he come across as childish to you? The summer break will come none too soon, and the separation will be good. Father has already booked my ticket to England. I'll have the whole summer to distract me and come back with a clearer head."

Even having prior knowledge of the pending English holiday, I still felt the tremor in my soul from the shock of it all. Time passed too fast, and here it was but ten weeks away. My precious young lady would be gone the entire summer. What wonders of the world might she encounter? The annual family visit only lasted two weeks but now that Mother was no longer here, the dynamics had changed. Two weeks was tolerable, at best, and I did not want to contemplate three months. Oh, dread of it all! Just the thought was mere torture.

She tilted her head and took on a weightier countenance. "Sebastian, are you all right? You look peaked, almost green, but how —"

It made me laugh slightly. "Dearest, you know I cannot be sickly. Am I not morte, dead, without life? No, my lovely, but thank you for caring."

She climbed out of bed, stood directly in front of me, and gazed into my eyes. "Well, it is more than obvious something is not right with you." Her combative attitude could be wearisome, but I reveled in the challenge of matching wits with the feisty creature. I walked straight through her despite the odd buzzing it made in my essence. Turning on her heel, "that, sir, was like cheating, but it did tickle me and not my stomach." She raised her eyebrows and flirtatiously giggled, knowing full well how uncomfortable such a comment made me feel. Yes, I do believe this old essence had developed feelings in all manners of emotion. All I lacked was the act of touching—physical sensation.

There was a tap on her bedroom door. In a hushed voice, "Devon, are you awake?" What was this? Was Father testing to see if she was awake? I checked out the hall, and the blonde was nowhere in sight.

"Yes. Come in."

"I had a wonderful night with you at the game. We must have outings together. Just us." He sat on the side of her bed, petting her hair. "I hope my, er, um, closeness with Cecilia has not created a divide between us."

She took his hand, and with a warm, loving smile, she answered. "Father, of course not." I could feel the electricity in the air. Something was brewing. "Whom you decide to make out with is your business, just as whom I decide to make out with is mine." She looked him squarely in the eyes. "Fair warning, though, I will kick up a stink if you take someone to bed while I am in the house. Are we clear? I feel confident you would not want to bear witness if I entertained in my bedroom." Silence. Father's face bore a look of utter shock and horror. "Calm down. Just yanking your chain! I'm not one of those girls, no worries." She delightfully giggled. "Now, cart your butt to bed, but first wash. You smell of her perfume." He kissed her forehead and bid her good night.

All in a Dream

Days turned into weeks; before I knew it, she was packing her trunk for a summer holiday in England. I had three days with her to myself, and we had been enjoying nightly dream strolls. We chatted, pondered, laughed, and cried. She was part of me, and I of her. After what seemed like hours of packing, she bathed and climbed into bed. As she slept, I lay by her watching each breath. At the first few twitches of her eyelids, I strolled into her dream. She was seated on a red and white checked picnic cloth with a lovely basket of fruit, cheese, and a palette of meat rolled and held in place with silver picks. Truly idyllic.

Her eyes sparkled with joy when she gazed up at me. "I wondered if I would see you today, Sebastian." Her beauty was breathtaking. I lounged beside her propping my head in the palm of my hand. I twirled one of the silver picks in my mouth. Ever-so-delicately she slid it from my mouth and then pushed me on my back with great force. She straddled my hips grinding down on me for a kiss. My body responded uncontrollably. Breaking from our kiss, she quizzically looked into my eyes. "Is that what I think it is? That means you want to make love to me, right?"

Oh dear. Having been male, my body betrayed my thoughts on too many occasions while I was alive and now, even in death. I could not come up with a proper and polite answer for the life of me.

"Say something, anything." Her eyes were begging me.

"I will. It is a difficult question, my lovely."

"What's difficult? It's either yes or no." She could be stubborn and damn argumentative.

"Not that simple. The response is not my mind but my body, and only in a dream. We both know dreams are not true; they are only figments of our imagination." She held my shoulders down and put the weight of her body on mine, which did nothing but make the problem worse. "Of course, I want to make love to you, but I will not; you must understand. I do not wish to take your maidenhead. That is for your marriage night. I am perplexed why Mother did not tell you about it." I forced her from on top of me by rolling onto my side and sitting up.

She stood and began to walk away, suddenly turning with an expression of delightful discovery. With a hand on her hip, she spoke with an air of newfound wisdom. "Right you are, sir; dreams are figments of my imagination. What I do in my dreams is not and cannot be part of my actual life, right? So, if I wanted you to make love to me, you would have to because I am the author of my dreams. Food for thought, Sebastian, my wise old sage. Fear not; I will not make you do anything you do not wish to do, at least for now." I strolled out of the dream as quickly as I had entered it. She beckoned me back, apologizing all the while, but I was determined to make my exit, and I did.

Something was different about my precious lady. It was a side I was none too thrilled to see. I have always known she was sassy and opinionated, but I never thought of her as anything except a step above the rest. Perhaps the three months would be a good time for re-evaluating the twist in our friendship. Silly girl did not consider I was in control of everything in the house. I was the master of this domain, and I chose to walk or not walk in her dreams.

I stayed cloistered in the attic, still angered by Devon's manipulative airs. Time and again, she beckoned me to her. When the tears began falling from her wondrous violet eyes, I felt a crushing weight like that of a ship's anchor upon my chest. How was it that I felt emotion without a beating heart? Whether absurd or not, it was a fact I found interestingly disturbing. I could no longer refuse her.

"Yes, Devon?" I responded coldly.

She hung her head. "I have behaved poorly and taken our friendship for granted. Can you see your way to forgive me? I cannot leave with such a heavy heart, knowing I may have ruined our exquisite relationship." Her eyes glistened like the sun's magic upon the sea. I could see a trail of dried tears, which struck discord within me. It disheartened me to know I had pained her.

"Devon, all this confusion and blurred lines are a result of my unnatural desires. What's done is done and forgotten." I tucked three letters inside her bag. "There is a letter to be read the first day of the months you will be away. If you wish to write me, address the envelope in your name, and I will know. Feel no obligation to pen me. Enjoy your time in England, my dear. Bon Voyage and safe travels." She placed her arms around my essence, and while I was a mere vision, there was a distinct electricity between the two of us.

I heard Father coming up the stairs. "Devon?" He came across as cold-blooded. Maybe it was a matter of the English stiff upper lip, but I found the whole experience devoid of warmth and love. "Goodness, you have packed your entire wardrobe. You'll be gone only three months."

She gave a good eye roll, "Hardly my whole wardrobe, Father. I hope you will be able to manage."

He rolled his eyes back at her, which he exaggerated for a response. "Hardly." He took the cases downstairs. "Be quick, Devon. I'm afraid we'll encounter heavy traffic, and you must be there two hours before, you know." And that was that.

With Father downstairs, I made my appearance. "I shall miss you, Sebastian. If only you could come with me. I know you would love Chelsea and my family." While I could hear the excitement in her voice regarding her travels, I could also see the sadness in her eyes and hear a sniffle or two.

Quickly she descended the stairs shouting farewell to the house, but I knew it was meant for me.

I was equally as curious about Father's actions whilst Devon was away. Perhaps I would glean insight into what made the man tick. I found myself doing the same old routine I had done for the past century— staring hours on end out of the lounge window, wondering what sort of journey the souls passing by might encounter.

Making my rounds through the house, I found myself in Devon's room. Her scent lingered in the chamber. Resting in her bed, I found an array of images floating by my mind's eye, each more pathological and disturbing than the previous. A debate ensued within my own mind trying to ascertain a logical reason that argued the outcome, damage, and sweetness of being with my lovely Devon as a man and woman. It would be but a mere dream and not alter her virginity. The thought in itself, while intriguing, was on a whole new level of absurdity and derangement.

I heard the front door slowly open, followed by a whispered call, "Nell." All remained quiet. I already knew Nell had retired from the day and was well on her way home. Snickers and giggled whispers caught my attention. I fully expected to see Wills' mother but instead, I was shocked to see a young lady, maybe twenty-one, with dark hair streaked with purple. She was giggly in a false manner and had a mouth even a sailor would not claim. I supposed, in a harlot kind of way, I found some attractiveness. When she started disrobing, groping him from room to room, she left a wake of cheap clothing— time for me to retire. *Really Father* was all I thought. Girls such as this were certainly from a house of women with loose morals billing by the hour or the service. I was pleased to see he drew the line at smoking in the house. Dreadful! Yes, it was time for me to skulk my way to the attic.

❦

The days passed as slowly as a snail's pace. I missed my precious treasure beyond any scope of reason. The time away from Devon was not good for my essence. I found myself remembering all the horrid deeds I had done whilst a devilish young lad and was unabashedly ashamed. I wasn't doing anything different than other lads; I was merely more skilled and perhaps a bigger scoundrel. What were the lads like approaching my sweet Devon, and would she be wise to their schemes and blatant lies? Time would tell.

It had been only three weeks, yet the postman delivered the first letter from my treasure. I slipped it from the collection of daily mail. I was consumed with intrigue and excitement.

My darling Sebastian,

I miss you more than I would have ever guessed, but there is much news from this side of the pond. Mother lives in a grand old townhouse close to the Knightsbridge tube, which is very convenient. It is all you would think it to be, knowing Mother. However, it is the only thing here resembling Mother. The change is marvelous. She has easily gained one, maybe even two stones and looks smashing. She no longer wears a sad expression but rather one to be described as perky and girlish. But, and hold on to your hat, the most significant addition to her life is Sean, her live-in boyfriend. Yes, you read that right. He is a fiery-haired Irish whiskey merchant. Quite tall and strapping, the two of them make a lovely couple. There is much joy and flirtation between the two. Honestly, I have not ever seen Mother happier. Now that I have dropped the bombshell, the rest is relatively mundane.

I have reconnected with some of the girls I used to know and have had fun adventures with them. I have taken to a boy, Baron O'Brien; yes, he's from Ireland. His father relocated from Dublin to London. He has an absolutely brilliant personality with a sharp sense of humor, staggering looks, and charm.

From what the girls have told me, he has yet to have a serious girlfriend, but many dates and many girls. I can hear you right now telling me to be cautious and perhaps wary of his motives.

She was most correct. I have known many boys and men to chat up the ladies only as a notch on their belt. Admittedly I, too, had played Jack the Lad a few times in my misspent youth.

Sebastian, I wish you could be with me. You would love it. I have had a few cherished days with Grandmother. I must confess, I told her about you. Everything. We had quite an interesting conversation about dream walking and its potential, almost like a secret affair. Do not be sore with me. She had a spirit living with her, or I guess she lives with the spirit. She gets it, but the girl has never dream walked.

I guessed not. The girl did not have a most unholy obsession with Grandmother. How desperately I wanted to kiss Devon, hold her, and never let go. I surprised myself with how much I, too, pined for her. I hoped her love interest remained a gentleman with my precious darling.

Those are all the juicy bits. I must close for now, but I will write again with any updates.

I love you, Sebastian, with all my heart.

She did not sign off, but those three little words echoed in my heart. Nothing else mattered. I had another two-plus months to ponder our relationship. As much as I would like to say the days flew by, they certainly did not. The only activity was the parade of girls and women to grace our home. Father was quite an amorous man. I barely recognized the man who sat stiffly behind the financials peering over from time to time. One positive side effect of his almost scandalous behavior was he came out from the bottom of a bottle.

Time felt as though it were standing still. After the completion of the first month, I wondered if she would take time to read or even respond to my second letter. Thankfully within days of the beginning of the second month, the letter arrived.

Bonjour Sebastian, my treasure,

Hope this finds you content and not too lonesome for me. Truthfully, I have been quite busy shopping and traveling with Grandmother. We spent three days in Paris. Grandmother met her special man-friend who took us to dinner—such a charmer with his heavy French accent. The second day he had his nephew, Antoine, escort me around the city. He is smashing and deliciously handsome. At the end of the day, which went late into the evening, I gave him a farewell kiss. I can hear you now, 'Devon, do not be so easy to succumb. Behave. Be a lady and play a little hard to get!' To wit, I respond, 'I'm living life to the fullest.' If I were of the male persuasion, Sebastian, you would not say the same thing. Probably more like a high-five and well done. Am I right, or am I right? I miss you to the point I get an ache in my stomach. I cannot wait until our lips can touch again. I hope Father is behaving. Until next time. I love you!

There it was again. Those three little words set my world alight. I poured over and over Devon's words. I, too, looked forward to the next time our lips met. The sheer memory of our kiss stirred something inside. It was pleasing to hear Grandmother still had romance in her life. Perhaps I was a tad jealous. The second letter, while most welcomed, created much food for thought. At some point, Miss Devon will meet the man of her dreams; they will court, marry, and have a family. What of old Sebastian? Would we forever share a secret affair of the heart? What a resplendent thought.

I sat on the settee, watching the stream of cars pass by. Off in the distance, I heard the timely clamoring of the streetcar. Punctual as usual, I listened as it approached – a most rickety clapping of years gone by. The cheerful ding as it came to a halt always seemed to lift my soul. It used to be gentlemen with satchels or briefcases going or coming from work. As the years passed and changed, I found the passengers were more of the fairer sex than before, perhaps because of the war. Presently, while there were still lovely people coming and going, the passengers had more of a ruffian appearance. I could only think, *what a shame.* Some of the gentility and loveliness had been cast to the wayside. The last person to exit was none other than Miss Purple Hair herself. Oh dear, I certainly hoped Father would not be entertaining her this evening.

Up she strutted to the front door, she and her attitude. She rang the doorbell and banged on the door. *Hmm.* Nellie, who had been preparing to leave for the evening, opened the door. "Hello. May I help you?"

"I need to see Ian." She was common and gruff.

"I'm terribly sorry, but Mister Ian has not returned from work yet. May I leave a message, or perhaps you could leave me your card, and I shall set it aside for him."

"No, lady, I'll just wait inside." She started to shove on the door.

Nellie stood firm but held a smile. "I'm sorry, dear, but perhaps you should call him or come back later."

The girl pushed harder. "I didn't come all this way to wait outside. I have called, and he hasn't answered or called back. This is my last effort before I slam him with a paternity suit. I'm sure he wouldn't want that!" She threw her body weight into the door, jolting Nellie back a step. I rushed to the door and conjured up all my wherewithal, forcing the door closed. Nellie bolted it and went to the phone.

"Sorry to bother you, sir, but there's been an incident at the house. A young girl came to the house looking for you and tried to force her way inside after I said you were not home. She is sitting on the front steps, refusing to move. Shall I call the police, sir?" She waited as he responded. "I will wait until you get home, sir. Are you certain you wish for her to be let in? Very well, then."

Once the call had ended, Nellie opened the door and welcomed the girl inside. It was clear as glass this was not to Nellie's liking, nor mine, may I add.

Nellie approached the young woman. "Would you care for a cold drink or some water while you wait? Mister Ian should be home shortly."

"No, but if you have a beer, I'll take one of them." She looked blankly at Nellie.

"I am afraid we are all out of beer and did you not say something regarding pregnancy?" I had forgotten Nell's proclivity for slicing sarcasm. Well done, yes indeed, well done.

The trollop had a surly, distasteful countenance. Father must have been well intoxicated to invite such a person into his home. With a nasty squint of the eyes, she responded. "Coke will do, then."

If my understanding were to be correct, I could not help but feel genuinely sorry for the baby with a mother like the purple-haired harlot. After being served her beverage, there was a pause left open for a word of gratitude, but ne'er a thank you or kindness to Nell. I supposed I should not be surprised, yet, people and their ill ways had taken me off guard on many occasions. She strolled around the lounge, picking up everything. I waited to see if she pocketed any of the Hurstall's trinkets. With the grace of a three-legged dog, she managed to spill her drink as it rolled up the side of the glass and splashed onto the antique Oriental rug. It was apparent she had not one thought of cleaning the mishap – merely smudged it in with her toe.

Hearing the back door close delighted my ears. Father was home, and certainly, he would throw her out on her ear.

"Welcome home, sir. Now that you are here, I will start home if that is all right with you." She all but curtsied; Nell was not herself; it was apparent the girl had shaken her to the inner core.

He poured himself a drink and entered the lounge. The girl turned abruptly as Father stood in front of his usual chair. "Please take a seat. I understand you wish to speak with me." She managed to slump onto the settee with a snide look. I remembered thinking she was fairly attractive in a cheap kind of way; however, the closer I looked, the more slovenly she looked.

71

"You got dat right, Ian. I'm pregnant, and you're the pops. Whatcha gonna do for me and the kid?"

Father looked at her with his air of confidence, and if I must say, he may have worn a slightly amused expression as he swirled the contents of his glass around. "Stacy, while our one encounter was entertaining, it is with certainty I say to you I am not the Father. It is quite an impossibility, you see. Soon after my daughter was born, I sustained an accident rendering me unable to produce any other offspring, sadly, I must say. I would have enjoyed having more children, but I wish you the best of luck and congratulations on your being with child." He took the last swallow of his drink and rose. "It was a pleasure visiting with you. Do you require cab fare?"

Well done, Father, yes, well done. The little she-devil would have to corner one of her other lovers du jour. Sad, indeed, for Mother and Father, but Miss Devon took the energy of two or three children. Indeed.

My goodness, the girl had a mouth on her. She called Father every nasty term one could contemplate. In a huff, she stood, turned to Father, and with a most distasteful look on her face, she threatened to sue him.

Father merely walked to the front door and opened it, indicating he wished her to leave. The venom of her tone of voice was almost frightening. I made a mental note to lock and batten down the hatches every night; I would not put anything past this creature. Even though it was an unpleasant circumstance, I must admit there was a thrill all the same. It added a new dimension to the everyday mundane existence.

Father poured another drink and seemed a tad melancholy as he sat sipping from the glass. He pulled out his phone and placed a call. He looked at his watch. "Oh my, it's one in the morning." Evidently, the person picked up. "So sorry, old chap, I forgot the time difference. Do pardon me; I shall ring back in the morning. I am completely forgetting myself. This is Ian Hurstall. Please excuse the—" The person on the other side of the call must have told him to hold on. Moments later, his face brightened, and his eyes sparkled.

"Devon, it is good to hear your voice. I miss you terribly, darling. The house is void of life and laughter without you. How are you getting on?" I could hear her lovely voice. The words were unclear, but she rattled on for nearly half an hour. Father held onto her every word smiling all the while. His smiles and happiness filled my soul, and I missed her with every part of my essence. "Certainly, darling, you can come home early. Please tell me when and I shall change the ticket. But, of course, you are most capable of doing so yourself. Call with the date and time, and I will be at the airport to greet you." I felt like a child on Christmas. My precious was returning to me earlier than expected. The news was most exhilarating. "I see no reason why your friend cannot stay here. As you know, we have ample room. What is her name? Do I know her parents?" There was a moment of silence. "Hm. No, no problem, darling. Baron is his name, you say? Very well, an Irishman at that." Father took in a deep breath, slowly letting it out so as to go unnoticed. While Father agreed to the arrangement, I certainly did not. She was far too young to have a male companion stay under the same roof. What was Father thinking? They ended the call with an exchange of love, well wishes, and anticipation of seeing one another. "Bye and good night, my darling."

CBaron

While it was delightful to hear her voice, my thoughts were consumed with the Baron fellow. She must be taken quite strongly by him to extend an invitation to her home. Baron! The idea of him sickened me even though I had no notion of him other than Devon's fondness for him. A retreat to the attic beckoned.

I sat at the secretary intending to compose a flirtatious, undeniable statement of adoration and love on the odd chance it would bring our frolics inside her dreams to her mind. My thoughts of the young beauty brought an imagined warmth and longing, followed by pangs of jealous torment. If I had not already taken a dive over the banister in grief and rage more than a century prior, I could easily see where these new thoughts of jealousy might compel such dramatic action. The pace of plotting had commenced and increased. My lovely had threatened me with seduction amidst her dream. *Hmm.* My thoughts, while unnatural, perhaps perverse, were conjured in my mind. Consumed with the pleasures I could deliver, prying her from this Baron fellow into my arms thrust me into a swirling dark void. I knew I was on the edge of the grace bestowed upon my wretched soul teetering to the point I might fall into the abyss and lose my connection to a life, her life. I had crossed the brink and could see where my soul was merging with madness. Stop this at once; I cried to myself.

I hadn't realized the night had fled until I heard Nellie as she entered through the back door. Father was still in his own swell of dreams whilst reclining in an armchair behind his desk in the study. Just a peek, an invisible pry to see what paths of uncertainty the conversation with Devon had provoked. To my shock and somewhat dismay, Father was dreaming of a meeting with business contacts and had nothing to do with my darling. Really Father, where is your creativity? I must have disturbed him; he woke just as I strolled out of his dream. He stood and stretched; arms held high. He quickly retired to his chamber, showered, dressed, and snatched a pastry as he left for work.

Busy in the kitchen, Nell had begun preparing the trappings of dinner, and I felt confident the aromas were indicative of the sumptuous taste to follow later in the evening. I sat for some time observing. Half an hour into my voyeurism, Nell spoke aloud. "You're not the only one missing her, ya know?" I stepped into the dining room, then the study. Who on earth was she talking to? Surely not me, and Father had already left. The home was absent of any other presence. Odd, she had never been one to talk to herself. "I'm not bothered one way or the other; speak to me or not. Show yourself or not. I know full well you're traipsing around here. Whoever you are, your presence is getting stronger. Maybe anger, sadness. Whatever your feelings, my ghostly friend, they have become much stronger. I don't think Mister Ian would find having a spirit in the house very amusing and may just up and sell, and then you'd lose your Devon forever." To my utter shock, she was addressing me. Retreat! Retreat! Off to the attic, I escaped.

Sitting at the secretary, I decided to pen my thoughts.

My Darling Devon,
I have kept a dull ache within the cavity of my being since your departure to England. I look forward to the time when we may meet again. From what

I've gathered, you shall be returning with a guest. Soon we can once again spend time together sparring wits. All have greatly missed your countenance. Speaking of all, my darling, have you spoken to Nell about our time together or mentioned my residence? I was most perplexed this morning. Our merry housekeeper addressed me aloud. Apparently, she felt my essence. I find this most peculiar as this was the first time. Perhaps my excitement regarding your return heightened my energy, making it palpable to others. I must remember this in the future. I would be ever so despondent if Father decided to sell our home due to fear of spirits.

Regarding one of our last conversations before your departure, I have given much thought to the topic of intimacy. This old soul just may surprise you with a trick or two. I will give not one more hint and let it remain a surprise. All my love and devotion, my darling.

Sebastian

I felt like a proud beast with a puffed-up chest. Who would have ever thought machismo could enter the realm of a spirit's life? A tingle in my lips moved lower and lower on my body, and I knew at this very moment I wanted Miss Devon in a most carnal manner. Come home, my sweet, and dream, dream, dream. Truly, I wanted her more than anything, even life. Once in slumber, she would have the embodiment of my soul.

Later in the week, the news came as such a welcome surprise. My dearest Miss Devon was returning home late the following week, only days until she was mine again. The more I thought about her return, the more excited I felt. Pacing in the attic, I began a pursuit of truth. Examining oneself, quite often, was a most painful journey. At this point, I admitted I had let any sense of reason disappear. I knew full well it was said absence made the heart grow fonder, but this incessant whine of mine was beyond all compare. Had I fallen in love with that which would and could never be mine, or was this mere substitution for the true love of my life who mingled along the streets of gold with the like of angels and saints? I pondered what may have become of her father. He was such an ill-mannered, hypocritical brute.

As part of the bourgeoisie, one would have assumed he held poise, grace, and gentlemanly sophistication. Nothing could be further from the truth. I witnessed his cruelty with his wife, and then I felt the crumble inside my soul.

I knew better than to be in Scarlet's bedchamber. Her parents were across town and would not return until much later. The servants had already turned in for the night; besides, I knew they were quite fond of me. Skin tones were darker, much darker than mine; they still considered me one of their own. They had personally felt the cruel hand of their owner. On more than one occasion, Rufus had forewarned me of their early return, saving me from being caught in a most compromising embrace. I dread to think of what might have befallen my lovely Scarlet.

Although French by birth, my family had emigrated to America, Boston, to be precise. We knew a life of wealth and prosperity. Although only an eighteen-year-old lad, my parents had made certain I had the appearance of polish and fine grooming. I knew many families found me a most suitable catch for their daughters and orchestrated our, by all appearance, happenstance meetings. Immature sensibility, unfortunately, led me to take advantage of the willingness of the young maidens. My parents would have held their heads in shame had they had any idea of my fornication. Maybe, just maybe, this was the ideology behind my immediate disdain for Baron O'Brien. I only hoped I did not have to tolerate a thick Irish dialect. Poor lad, I was already pitting against him and had not even had a single encounter with him.

The minutes turned into hours which turned into days, and finally, yes, finally, t'was the day my treasure would return to me. My impatience was most bothersome and seemed to mount with each passing moment. I paced the floors, once again, like an expectant father. At last, the sound I had awaited. Devon's voice carried through the house as she, Father, and the boy entered. It was most apparent she had been in England as her crisp accent was even richer than I remembered if that were at all possible. The difference in her inflections seized my heart whilst heating my admitted depravity. Time had not lessened my amorous feelings and desires. *Calm down, boy*, I said to myself.

"Mr. Hurstall, sir, I'd be more than happy to carry the cases in from—" he paused as Devon raised an eyebrow directed at him. *What a brown-nose!* I loved the description Devon had used many times. It certainly painted quite a picture and was most applicable in this obnoxious situation. I allowed my essence to circle the intruder, getting an up-close point of view. His eyes did not reveal impostor, but the voice and the way in which he carried himself said otherwise. Perhaps the lad was nervous; he was definitely out of his element or, as one might refer, a fish out of water. Folding my arms, I stood to the side and found myself judging his every movement. I lingered for a brief self-scolding. Miss Devon most assuredly would have chastised me for being critical and less than welcoming of her guest.

"Baron, I'm most capable of carrying my own." Did my precious already seem chapped by the lad? Perhaps it was merely hopeful thinking on my behalf. She had been most correct in her description of him and not blinded by affection. The lad was striking and had the stature of Adonis. She led him into one of the guest chambers. "This is where you'll be sleeping. You may consider it your bedroom; mine is just down the hall. I've been dying to do this since we landed." She wrapped her arms around the boy's neck and passionately kissed him.

The cad held her embrace tightly in one arm while the free hand attempted to navigate her body. I could not tolerate one more second of this and shoved a stack of magazines from atop the nightstand. Ol' Baron leapt nearly out of his skin. *Oh, this was going to be fun*, I smiled to myself. Devon glanced quickly in my direction, knowing full well I had been the culprit behind the slight disturbance. The expression on her face did not give this old soul comfort. If anything, I felt dressed down and ashamed.

Perhaps it best I retire to the attic and not torture myself with her wanton advances upon the lad. Could I blame him for accepting her affection and responding with his own passion? Miss Devon was ravishing, and I, too, had the same desire as our houseguest. Like being drawn to a horrible train wreck, I could not stop watching, no matter the consequence to my already broken heart.

"Lass, now that I have you on your home turf, might we take our adventures a little further?" He raised an eyebrow and rendered a cheeky smile while grabbing her backside, drawing her into him. For a mere moment, I felt insane with anger, or was it jealousy? Where the hell was Father? Was he going to let this disrespect go unawares? By God, this was most negligent on his behalf to allow his precious Devon alone with the rascal. *Yes*, I heard Father as he ascended the stairs. *Ah, keep it up, my boy*, I thought. Hopefully, he will be caught in the act. Father will set him straight, maybe even give him a thump or two. One could hardly blame him.

Once he topped the stairs, Father called aloud. "Knock, knock, you two." Pardon me? A warning? Father had assuredly lost his wits. What was he doing, condoning some sort of randy behavior? Oh, dear, Father had no idea he was throwing his sweet lamb to the wolf. I was not going to have any part of the decadence. I would protect our girl's honor and reputation. As I could easily walk in my girl's dreams, I could create havoc and fright in the young man. Father continued. "Empty your cases, Baron, into the bureau." Father looked in the wardrobe. "If you need more clothes hangers, I have stacks. Just let me know." At least the lad had enough respect, or was it savvy to step away from Devon whilst Father was in the guest chamber. To avoid more irritation on my part, I fled to the attic.

Picking up the pen, I began my letter. I realized I needed to calm myself, as it took three times trying before my words took on a more civil tone.

My Dearest Devon,

Welcome home, my darling. I have missed you immensely. Baron is precisely what you portrayed in your letters: strikingly handsome and a strapping lad, he is indeed. From first appearances, he seems enamored with you. You, too, seem taken with the lad. Bully for you!

I read over the words, and once again, the tone hardly shone me in the best light. Dear me, yet another scrapped attempt. My thoughts were interrupted as I heard her beckon for me.

"Sebastian, I know you're around here somewhere. Aren't you going to welcome me home?" I watched as she paced her floor, looking at the ceiling.

I went right behind her as close as possible without actually touching her; otherwise, she may have perceived our electrical current. "Welcome home, my dear! You look radiant." I cocked my head to one side blasting forth the warmest smile I could muster.

In a flash, she spun around, bearing a bright, beautiful bow-like smile. If I had a beating heart, it would have echoed throughout the house. "I told Baron I needed a short nap from our long flight. I thought you might want to join me. Oh, and you're a bit dramatic, Sebastian. Pushing the magazines to the floor. Really!" Touching her bottom lip with her index finger, her eyes sparkled with a sassy twinkle. "Temper tantrums do not suit you, nor jealousy. Don't you know by now? You are the man of my dreams and can never be replaced, silly!" Slowly she began to undress. Instinctively I turned my back. "For Heaven's sake, are you giving the pretense that you have never watched me undress or seen my naked body? For Heaven's sake, Sebastian!" She sounded annoyed.

Still, with my back turned, I succinctly spoke. "It may come to your surprise, but I have never watched you disrobe, nor have I viewed your unclothed body. I have more scruples than to sneak a peek. Just the thought makes me feel lecherous, my dear."

She giggled, spinning around me in all her beautiful nakedness. I caught a glimpse but closed my eyes with force and quickly, which made her laugh even more. She stood close, near enough that our energy charged in a spontaneous burst. The ignition ran the length of my body, causing an uncomfortable and unholy shiver. "Sebastian, you are such a prude!"

81

Eyes still masked by my eyelids, I emphatically refuted. "No, Devon, I am a gentleman. There is a big difference between a prude and a gentleman. I assure you, prude, I am not!"

With a look of disappointment, the same one she had at eight years of age, she drew her bedding back and climbed in. "Join me if you wish or not." The thick fringe of black lashes veiled her exquisite violet eyes. After several moments her breathing turned into a soft, whispered hush as she drifted to sleep. I knew it would not be long until tiny twitches of the eyes would indicate her nearing the land of Nod and my opportunity to walk with her, hold her and, yes, kiss her most luscious pouty lips. She clearly was exhausted, and sleep came upon her as effortlessly as drawing a sash.

Silently I entered her dream and hid out of view. She was on a park bench waiting for something or someone. I, too, waited. I did not want to be too brazen, thinking she was waiting for me when only a room away slept her latest attraction, but she had said clearly I was the man of her dreams.

I stealthily went to her and placed a sweet but arousing kiss behind her right ear. Her shoulders dropped as she tipped her head to the side, broadening the canvas of her neck for a bath of kisses. She took my right hand from her shoulder, slid it inside her blouse, and placed it upon her breast. Her hand atop mine gave her control to tighten the grasp. Speaking honestly, I did not even try to feign a struggle. Her skin felt like the softest silk begging to be experienced, eliciting a purr of delight from the innermost part of her being. Was my precious darling a woman now? Had she been deflowered whilst in England? Clearly, the lad in the next room over had not tasted the spoils judging from his earlier comment. "Sebastian, I have been waiting for you. Take me, all of me. I have waited patiently. Here, come." She took my hand and led me around the park bench to an isolated area amidst a glen of trees.

The arbor provided a garden of Eden for her and me. She kissed me, sparing no expense with her love. I felt my clothing being peeled from my body as she explored my being and the secrets beneath. What was I to do? I knew full well what I desired, but what would be more prudent? Just in that one thought, the words rang out and said it all. Had I become a reclusive prude? Please, God, no! I threw caution to the wind, determined to fulfill her every fantasy.

Her clothing faded away as willed by her dream, and I gave in to her, and yes, my wiles, as well. We coupled a most passionate and beautiful duet. My passion burned brightly with intensity met by her willingness and desire. How long had it been since I poured myself into a loving embrace? My precious, dearest darling demanded my best performance, and I heartily accepted the challenge. We sighed in perfect synchrony as I rolled onto my side. Pure euphoria. She smiled at me, revealing the deepest emotion she held captive in her heart. "Sebastian, you are the man of my dreams. Your love-making skills were all I could possibly have imagined. And for you, my sexy-spirited amore, did I fulfill all your fantasies? I know I'm not Scarlet, but I genuinely love you and wish only to please you."

While her words were tender and the moment pristine, like out of a great romance story, I knew in the corners of my mind I had carried out the greatest of injustices. How could I profess my love to her and yet betray her? Yes, it was glorious to be loved in such a manner, but what door had I selfishly opened? I held her in my arms and delicately kissed her forehead, running my fingers through her hair. My God, such a tumult of emotion. It had been nigh on a century and a half at least since I had been loved as deeply. Now that we had traversed this path, where would it lead? Where could it possibly lead? I answered my own ponderance. Nowhere, that's where. Things were much simpler when I could enjoy her spoiled tantrums, canny precocious thoughts, and amusing childish threats. Would I one day be tossed irrelevant like dear Charlotte, the stuffed bear?

All these thoughts battered to the forefront of my mind as I lost myself in her gaze, twining her lovely locks around my fingers as though trilling an invisible flute. I traced the lines of her face. "You are exquisite in every possible way, my heart, my love."

"Then why do you look almost melancholy?" she asked with heartfelt truth. The thought of my feelings was real to her and seemingly of grave importance. My reply must be well thought out and with wisdom, a key ingredient I somehow had abandoned like a worn-out blanket or shoe full of holes.

My words must ring with honesty. "Regrettably, I am remiss with what to say." I fell silent, looking deep into her magnificent pools of violet fringed by a fan of black lashes.

Confusion registered upon her countenance as glistening tears formed in the wells of her eyes. "What's wrong? Is it me?" A single tear spilled over the edge and slowly began its course down her cheek. More would soon follow if I did not get this situation under control. I do not know where this plight should have rested, but it certainly was not with tears from my most precious beloved.

"No, no, no, Devon. Exquisite does not even begin to describe you, your body, and the pleasures you bestowed upon me. I am but a foolish soul wanting that which is not mine to take. I most assuredly love you but am unable to offer anything but love in a dream." My eyes cast downward whilst my very essence shuddered in shame.

Devon stretched her neck from side to side, maintaining an undisturbed focus on my eyes as though contemplating the words and meaning behind my bewildering thoughts. Truth be spoken, I was but a restless soul, empty and lifeless, with nothing of substance to offer. It was as if she had breathed a second life filled with joy and happiness into me, yet it was all an illusion. I was incapable in my state of being more, a jagged pill to swallow. Were it possible to bring upon death twice, I would gladly step into those flames rather than bring sadness and misery to my dearest Devon. Placing my hands delicately on her face, I drew her near me, kissing her succulent lips. "I'll see you in the morrow, my love," and slipped out post-haste.

Back in the attic, I reflected on the dream. Devious as I was, my thoughts started down a most unpleasantly scheming journey trying to bury my misdeeds in a web of deceit. What if I, when mentioned by Devon, took on a curious, unknowing expression? As I knew, she would want to speak of our tryst whilst I would play unawares and confused, denying any such rendezvous. Perhaps it was merely her own dream created exclusively in her subconscious. "Regrettably," I would say with a coy smile. My head hung, how appropriate, as my shoulders slumped, realizing I was the worst of any character. Here, I had ravished my young love, devoured by my own passion, and then to recoil and turn the tide onto her. What monstrous ghoul I had become, and all for what? I was, in fact, although most unholy, in love. The debate continued for hours until I was filled with fury and rage. Out of control, I began knocking over furniture and throwing boxes, my essence consumed with anger.

I heard the attic door open as Devon entered. "Stop this instant! What is wrong with you? If there was ever a doubt about your existence, it has been more than confirmed. Father, Nellie, and Baron are completely freaked out, Sebastian. I knew damn well what issues were present and, because of you, was forced to reveal the knowledge of you and calm their fears. What do you have to say for yourself? You know, Nellie already knew there was a spirit in the house. After all your sneaking and voyeuristic behavior, the cat is now, with your tantrum, as they say, out of the bag!" She stood like a spitfire with one hand on her hip and fearless anger in her eyes. "Father thinks I'm off the deep end, but no one could deny the bangs and booms from the attic. Whatever it is, I hope it's out of your system."

I slunk into the only upright chair. I knew I looked as pathetic as I felt. I simply said I had no answer to impart to her. Perhaps it best I be left alone to stew in my self-made misery. She turned on her heel and stormed back down the stairs. I recognized the thump of angered Devon steps all too well. While it had been most amusing at one time, it now served to push my soul deeper toward the pit.

Oh, The Sites

Days had gone by, and I still slumped in the chair. I had managed to upright and straighten the boxes, furniture, and destruction I had caused in the attic, but I was dejected. Would there be any room for forgiveness in her heart? I had to speak with her. I picked myself up, settled my hair, and retied my ribbon. My clothing never appeared disheveled; instead stayed in the original shape from whence I was laid to rest, yet I felt compelled to pull at my waistcoat.

Devon was stretching in bed, trying to cast off the sand from her eyes. After a few blinks, she seemed content. I cleared my throat to let her know I was getting ready to make an entrance. "Good morning, Sebastian. I hope you are in better spirits than the other day." Her voice lacked any warmth. "I have one question for you. Why did you stand me up when I waited for you on the park bench? I waited and waited, but no you. Why?"

I had the perfect opportunity to make up some excuses and be off the hook. She was none the wiser, but, alas, I would not. I sat on her bed, stroked her hand, or at least went through the motions. "My love, I came to your bench. Do you not remember? I kissed you first behind your ear

87

and then down your neck. We had a marvelous time together." She cocked her head with a look of absolute puzzlement in her eyes.

Like a child begging for a bedtime tale, she asked me to tell her about the dream. I was astonished, to say the least. Had she no memory of our intimacy? "My dear, I must admit my embarrassment and beg your forgiveness for my demonic episode of jealousy and unruly anger the other day in the attic. The thought of being with you in life is more than I can bear. You must know there can be no real outcome to an unnatural romance. While our kisses have been glorious, I fear anything other would only lead to disappointment." It was almost impossible for me to fathom her lack of knowledge regarding our most intimate moment together. Perhaps, should there be further interaction, would it, too, be non-existent in her memory? Fodder for the mind.

Devon sat amidst her covers, legs folded beneath her. "But, I love you, Sebastian. Do you not love me the same?" A single tear fell from her eyes as her breath hitched a sob. The feeling I had was that of a broken heart. I could not let this go unanswered. I tried to touch her cheek. I desperately wanted to take her in my arms and allay all her fears, yet, I knew I was the mastermind behind her sadness. If I could only wish back the time when she was a child, careful to observe but not get too close. She was the magnet drawing my soul. There was no denying it. How could our loving Creator allow this feeling to exist in my perilous non-existence? I felt a deep shudder in my essence.

"My precious Devon, I love you more than I can express or maybe more than you can comprehend." I knew my eyes had the look of forlorn. Could she not see how I loved her?

"But we kissed, and I felt it, and it was marvelous. Grandmother said there would be nothing wrong with an affair of the heart. Do you not believe in such?"

Before I could stop the words, they poured from my soul. "We made love, and it was euphoric, but you, for some reason, I know not why, cannot recollect the marvelous, magical experience." Her mouth dropped agape.

"When? When did this happen?"

"My love, while you slumbered from your journey. That very day you came home. I have felt so ashamed but took delight in your lack of remembrance. Perhaps t'was my guilt." She could not have had more shock register on her face than when I spoke those words.

"Perhaps, my ghostly amore, we need to pursue the avenue of romance once more and see if I am able to recall the interlude." She raised her eyebrows, smiled, and, as coy as a cat, whispered with amusement. "Sebastian, I mimic your tenor and brilliant old-world expressions when we speak. It is far different than the language of everyday slang I casually use with my friends. You speak with such eloquence and poise, and that's part of why I love you so." Having heard conversations on the television, I knew precisely the slang she referred to, and in my heart, I hoped she had not stooped to the level of ignorance and bawdiness of those on the screen. Perhaps my countenance reflected my thoughts; she giggled, "Oh, dear Sebastian, I am a teenager of this day and time, do not judge. I love our challenge of wit; it is such a rarity. Now, I must be going as not to be rude to my houseguest." She quickly changed as I fled to the rafters, then joined Father and Baron.

Father and Baron seemed, from all appearances, to get along well. From my point of view, Father had many openings to intellectually spar with the young man, yet he refrained. I guess, jolly good for him. Grumble. Grumble.

Devon skipped down the stairs. "Good morning!" She kissed Father on the top of his head and then, to my surprise, planted a kiss on young Baron's lips. I was shocked; Father gave no words of reproach for her inappropriate behavior. Still appalled, I sat in the corner of the room observing the idle chatter, begrudging Father's lack of command and Devon's lack of etiquette. "I hope you are well-rested. Baron, I'd love to take you around for a tour of New Orleans. We can start with a breakfast treat of beignets and coffee at Café du Monde, then wander the French Quarter for some window shopping. Then, we'll fly by the seat of our pants and see where we land."

Fly by the seat of our pants? Seat of our pants? What on earth did she mean by that? Was that her flighty use of the modern tongue? If so, I don't think I cared for it one bit. 'No, young lady,' Father should have said, 'what are your actual plans, none of this flying by the seat of your pants nonsense.' Wasn't he aware that this whimsical folly opened the door for inappropriate behavior and a welcome to ol' Baron to have his way with young Devon? No, sir, if Father wasn't going to step in and demand more explanation, I needed to thwart their departure, or at least try.

"Very well, then, you two, enjoy the sights. Devon, make sure your mobile is on and check in with me periodically. Without being too meddling, perhaps you might take Baron along the avenue to the river's bend and breakfast at Camellia Grill? That is truly an experience that many visitors are not privy to." Looking at the lad, Father commented, "It's a local favorite." Meddling? Has Father completely lost his sensibility? No, he must command with authority. What was this world coming to? Baron stood to leave with my princess, and I could not resist the urge to move, only slightly, the chair as to catch his ankle, but the boy was steady on his feet and laughed off his clumsiness. Devon looked toward the chair and tsked me. No one else knew it, but I did. Tsk, tsk indeed!

I sulked around the house the remainder of the day, only escaping to the attic to pen a quick note.

My darling,
Flying by the seat of your pants? How common and gauche. While the lad seems charming and sincere, remember he is a lad, and sometimes their actions and words may not be as transparent as they appear. Below the surface, I guarantee there are ulterior motives. I, too, was once young and equally as charming with my song-filled words and dandy smiles. Most lads are wolves in sheep's clothing, my dear. While I do not, in any way, dismiss your perception,

as you are and have always been most aware, you may get blinded by romance.

Tonight, you will not have to wait long on the park bench for my complete attention. I look forward to the promise of a wondrous walk amid your dream.

As always, I am deeply devoted to you.

Sebastian

Do I fancy myself too clever? My darling will undoubtedly see through my vain attempt at recapturing her attention. Perhaps it best if I remain at a distance and let this transient fascination with Baron run its course. In due time, the lad will strain her patience, and the closeness will fade. The question looming in my thoughts was the eventuality of the love of her life entering the picture. Wasn't her happiness the most important thing to me, not my misguided thoughts? Her fascination for me would surely dwindle with the passage of time, and her desire to have more in life blossom.

My essence started to feel weighted with guilt and sadness. Yes, the day would come when old Sebastian, the kindly spirit, would be a thing of her past, while my predicament, of my own device, would be eternal. Ne'er would she walk the halls with me kindred in spirit, nor did I relish a thought of her in my dreary, dismal existence. My heart was saddened. If only I could beseech my Creator to rip me from this limbo and let me walk the golden streets of eternity with my precious Scarlet, freeing me of my most unnatural and unholy obsession. In all His forgiveness, surely I could receive a pardon for the acts of a young, passionate, and foolish man. I sat with my eyes closed in remembrance of Scarlet's lovely golden locks and fairness of complexion. She was as though an angel walking on earth.

As quickly as those resplendent memories danced in my head, too, came the desire to witness her father wailing laments amidst the torturous flames of Hell. Was I so ghoulish to relish that thought? Perhaps, my Creator knew my innermost desire, thus making me an unwelcomed resident beyond the Heavenly Gate. Thoughts to ponder for the next hundred years, I suppose. The end of my imprisonment was well beyond any purview I possessed; indeed, my loving Creator would perhaps release me from my chains.

I read and re-read my letter to the dear one, postulating whether to put it amongst the daily post or tear it into tiny shreds. For once, I think I made the best choice and disposed of the evidence that may have shed a poor light on me, exposing my transparent manipulative nature. No, I chose to suffer in silence, maybe even sprinkle a bit of good cheer regarding young Baron. One day he would go the way of dear Charlotte, although never quite so loved.

The happy couple returned from touring the city. I pondered what activities I may have found disturbing, also contemplating the true nature of Baron—weaselly predator or a lad of a sincere heart? Judgment abated for the present. Father seemed joyful that the couple had returned safe and sound. I supposed he felt some brunt of responsibility for the safety of not only his cherished one but of the guest, as well.

"Devon, darling, would you and Baron like to dine with me tonight? I want to hear all about your adventures touring the city." Addressing the young man, Father continued the line of inquiry. "New Orleans is such a unique city, you must admit. Each part differs from the next, don't you find?"

"Yes, t'is, and your daughter is an excellent tour guide. She certainly showed me some interesting sights." I pursed my lips, crossing my arms over my chest, arching my back ever-so-slightly as though stanced and ready to request a duel. *Oh, no, young man!* I was not too fond of the double-entendre, and if Father didn't delve into the sights that seemed to enthrall Baron's young eyes, I most definitely would pry. I shook my head. Father could be so naïve at times, or did he blatantly choose not to go down that merry path? During the night, I would creep into the boy's head and pursue a proper interrogation. What harm could it do? A thorough questioning of the lad superseded my plan of a dream interlude with my darling.

"That would be lovely, Father, that is," she cocked her head to the side and smiled, "if Baron isn't too tired from today's activities." Catching herself, perhaps also a double-entendre, I was not thrilled by the conversation thus far. "We not only had breakfast at Camellia Grill, as you recommended, but I took him to the zoo and introduced him to sno-balls—" they both stuck their tongues out; hers was a vibrant green, and his a drab yellow. "I told him he should have tried the blue bubble gum, but Baron isn't very adventurous; however, he tasted my spearmint with condensed milk and had to admit it was smashing. Oh, what else did we do, hmm?" Yes, my dear, what else did the two of you do? What you described couldn't have occupied an entire day and exhausted the boy. A-hem. Do tell. "I completely forgot we drove to River Road to show him the levee." She giggled, obviously at the boy's expense. "Walking along the levee, Baron stepped in a pile of horse poop," and she laughed again. "You should have seen his face; it was hilarious."

"T'was funny. I trod right into a great heaping pile of sh—horse dung. I guess your daughter took mercy and brought me to a petrol stop so I could wash off me shoes and then for a sandwich fit to be a meal." He placed his hands gently on his stomach. "I'm bloody to the brim, I am." Okay, laddie, I see the path you're leading Father down. Maybe, the lad is too filled and unable to partake in a dinner invitation and must be left at the house alone with Devon? For the love of all that is good, Father, remove your blinders. " Devon warned me that New Orleans is a culinary experience and to expect to add some weight on my holiday. If she's not too tired, I'd totally get into more of the fine food." Grumble. What was it Devon called her schoolmates? Brown-nosers, and there it was for me to see - Baron of the Brown Nose.

After sitting and chatting, they all showered and dressed for dinner at Commander's Palace; ah, a restaurant held in high esteem. While it opened soon after my demise, I had overheard previous owners and their guests expound on legendary dishes fit for a king and service unsurpassed. It appeared Father was pulling out all the stops for this traveler. Hmpf. I grumbled my way to the attic.

Jealousy was not a feeling I'd had much experience with, perhaps because I always attained the interest of young ladies to my liking and had anything my heart desired. I dressed impeccably, suited in fashionable attire, with an abundance of coin filling my pockets. Frankly, until the Hurstalls bought the old house, I didn't care much about the owners. I supposed the elderly man was a tad interesting. I'd flit about, occasionally listen in on a conversation, and stick my nose in for local gossip, none truly worth the time of a listen, but there hadn't been life until that precious cherub entered the door. From the moment I laid eyes on her, I was delighted and completely enthralled. Despite maturing into an exquisite woman, she maintained her sassy attitude and opinionated way, and I loved it so.

I sat at the secretary, looking at a wordless page of stationery. The image, in itself, was a statement about my existence. Void. The countless faux-pas I had committed since the arrival of Miss Devon Hurstall were mounting daily. Still, the angry, jealous outburst in the attic, like that of a tortured demon, pained my soul. I felt ashamed, embarrassed, and void of anything resembling the man I once was. How utterly human I had become, and yet not in some ways, as I was long departed from life. I had the essential disadvantage of a missing heartbeat and a deep, illuminating breath. For the first time in perhaps a century, I succumbed to self-pity and loathing, and I was shattered to the deepest depths of my essence. All I needed was a mournful, dramatic *'woe is me'* to complete the misery.

Hours passed before Father, Devon, and Baron of the Brown Nose returned. To my utter disgust, both Father and our house guest were intoxicated to the point of slurring their words and stumbling along. My Miss Devon was perturbed beyond measure. *Boys, boys, you have made a grave mistake,* I thought, chuckling deviously to myself.

Stomp. Stomp. Stomp. Oh, how reminiscent of days gone by, but I knew the eventualities of these angered stomps. And yes, Devon threw herself on her bed and burst into tears. "Sebastian, I need you," she cried.

Sebastian to the rescue, my dear, I pompously thought and thanked the stars did not verbalize. With a saddened tone, I responded to her. "My sweetness, why on earth are you crying?" I knew too well, but it gave me a sincere drawing tone to coax her heartbreak into words.

"I want to go to sleep so that you can hold me. Father's too drunk, and Baron's an ass to even keep in conversation. I do not even want to look at him. Baron decided to match drink for drink with Father; yes, that's precisely what he did. We all know Father can easily fall into the bottom of a bottle. It did not take much for Baron to get Father on a roll. I hate how his common Irishness comes out when he drinks." She growled. "I am most annoyed and need to be in the company of a gentleman." Pierce my heart, me a gentleman? She wouldn't have thought so only moments ago when I was basking in darkness. Oh, my soul. Devon needed me now; therefore, it was not time to reveal the scoundrel I was and the horrible thoughts I was having. No, I'd be her gentleman, indeed.

"Lay rest your head, my dear. I'm sure neither Father nor Baron intended to upset you." I quickly turned my back to her as she peeled her clothes off, leaving them in a puddle on the floor. As she snuggled deep into her covers, I sat by her side. "There, there, my sweet, let slumber fall upon you, and I shall meet you in your dream." Tonight would not be the night to woo or take advantage of her sensitive feelings. I must remain a gentleman.

Her staggered whispered breaths slowly fell into a rhythmic balance as sleep and dreams began to steal her wakefulness. Straightening my waistcoat, I ventured forth. She was waiting on the park bench, still rattled with tears of disappointment. "Please hold me, Sebastian. I am so furious right now. All I can think of is hateful, horrible things to say to both Father and Baron, but that wouldn't be of benefit to anyone, now would it?" I sat beside her on the bench and was immediately consumed in her embrace. She clung to me like a frightened child, almost to the point of her body quaking. I stroked her hair, twining a long loose lock around my fingers. While not quite purring like a kitten, her sighs were indicative of one reaching calm and contentment. She filled my soul. "I love you, Sebastian," she cooed.

Desperately I prayed for the fortitude to advise her to abandon this unnatural complexity destined for disappointment, and to what end? For the present, my thoughts, while churning, kept a distance from my mouth. This shivering limpet of a wrought young lady was drastically out of character, so much so that I scarcely had words, merely silent strokes of love and compassion. I wasn't well enough acquainted with this Baron fellow to feel anything but anger and disgust, but Father, how beastly and shameful a performance. I mustered finally, "My precious love. Are we feeling a tad lighter? Let go of those angered thoughts; they are to no avail and will only perpetuate the distaste and pain you bear. Only you, my darling, have the power to forgive them and pass this unpleasantness by the wayside. I am sure Father will feel great regret and perhaps be a bit sheepish come morning. I cannot say what the remembrance or perception your young friend might use as an excuse or, perhaps, he may conjure an apology filled with sincerity. Being with you and Father in unfamiliar surroundings may have overwhelmed his common sense."

"Sebastian, have you ever been so angry there wasn't a word that could describe the feeling, yet your body took control and trembled as though it were your voice? You know, like the words were trapped by the vastness of the emotion shutting everything down except the energy to shake within violently?"

I held her still, attempting to calm her feelings. Had I felt so deep an anger, my yes, I wanted to answer her, but I knew it was not the forthright response at the moment. What should I say, 'yes, my darling, my anger shook so within that I saw my only release was to wrap bed linen around my neck and plunge over the second-floor banister. Thus being relegated, by my act of misadventure, to a sentence of eternity within the confines of the house.' I knew very well the power of anger. The memory was so clear I could conjure it up within a split second—beautiful Scarlet with twisted, broken limbs and blood trickling from her luscious mouth, dainty ears, and slightly upturned nose; the mask of death permanently upon her face. Her once sparkling eyes filled with curiosity snuffed with the clouded dullness of the absence of life. Those images were ever imprinted in my memory. I barely remember my demise. I can't recall pain from a broken neck or fear and dread of death approaching. No, I was consumed with that horrible image of my most precious Scarlet. A subject young Devon and I never broached and hoped we never would. She, quite aware of the broad strokes, never glinted at the details of the grotesque atrocity I had committed.

She slumbered in my arms amidst her dream. Gently I kissed her hair, lightly touching my lips to her mahogany locks. She stirred and turned in my arms, reaching to my face fulfilling the moment into a most passionate kiss. While the urge to continue this splendor, I pulled away. "You need rest, my dear. I will not allow my carnal senses to requite your anger with lust. While you are desirable in every way, I fear it is not the time and would result in even more complex feelings for you in the morning. Let us enjoy this intimacy of our embrace." Who had I become? Although twenty-one at my death, perhaps the years of watching life come and go had mellowed me to the point of an old soul. The strong desire to take Miss Devon up on her offer and parlaying it into an intertwining of our bodies had become controlled, subdued, and appropriated. Our impulses would serve better in another dream.

Operation Rescue

The morning rang in, and as I suspected, my young friend was still disappointed but no longer crazed with anger. Her sensibilities had returned, and her sharp, blade-like tongue was poised and ready for battle should anyone step in the wrong direction.

It was most apparent that Father felt ill, suffering from a bad head and queasy stomach, as he had one hand on his forehead and the other on his gut. I had no sympathy for the man. None at all. *Shame on you, Father. Shame. Shame.* "Devon, darling, could you serve up a spot of tea for me and perhaps a slice of toast lightly buttered?" I could barely believe my ears. Had Father lost his mind? He was the one that should be preparing a spot of tea and serving the saddened Miss Devon. *Tsk.*

She smiled with a half-cock to her lips. I waited; there was no doubt something laced with sarcasm was about to emerge. "Would you care for that with a helping of whiskey mixed in the tea or the whiskey merely straight up, is it?" A blow to Father, yes, but there was so much more she could have spewed, cutting him right at the knees, and he knew it. She cleared her throat as she made her way to the kettle. "Father, how about a slab of fried bacon topped with a slightly done egg? You know, sunnyside up and all runny?" I felt the slight breeze of insult mounting and the hurricane force mixed in the waters for a hell of a storm. Taking the chance, I appeared to her in the kitchen. She was startled at first, but then a wicked smile crossed her lips. I merely shook my head and mouthed, 'No.' That devilish twinkle acknowledged my sentiment, but she would have her say, one way or another. I heard clumsy steps coming toward the kitchen. I vanished.

"Mornin', love. Perhaps a bit o' tail o' the dog might be in order this mornin'." Her gaze was enough to knock over a wall of stone. *No, laddie, no,* I thought. Apparently, he had not seen the sharp snake-like strikes of our beautiful creature. His hair was straight up in the back, fanned like a peacock, and he was attired in baggy wrinkled pants, a cotton shirt ragged with holes, and bare feet. Where on earth had she found this bedraggled poor excuse for a lad? I've heard it told that some ladies are attracted to a bad boy, but this slovenly heap of excrement needed to get back on the potato boat post haste.

"Tail of the dog, you say. What is that to mean?" She stood with a hand on her hip.

"A wee sip of whiskey, my darlin'," he said with a most casual wink. He approached her with a look I did not care for in the slightest and had a mind to hit him in the head with the kettle.

She raised an eyebrow. For Miss Devon, that was like pulling back the bow and lining up the arrow. "I beg your pardon, but, firstly, you can get yourself back upstairs, shower because you reek of whiskey, dress in some proper clothes, take an aspirin or two, and return when you are fit to be in my presence. I don't know what kennel you were raised in, but that is how things are done in my home!" There was a look of shock on Baron's face; he slouched and shuffled back up the stairs, tail between the legs. The only tail he would sport that morning.

Devon brought Father his tea and sat in the chair to his left, not her usual spot. With pursed lips and squinty eyes at the ready to hurl daggers, she began to speak in a clipped, yet soft, tone. "Father, the incident of last night shall never be repeated. Do I make myself clear? I nearly called a cab for myself, leaving you, your lady friend, and Baron to fend for yourselves. How dare you speak like you're hanging with the boys in front of me, and if you wish to kiss your dates, I expect it to be in the privacy of your home and not in front of my friend or me. You encouraged Baron to act the same way. Utterly disgusting; you are my father. The one to protect my innocence. I am not accustomed to being treated like a common slut, nor will I tolerate your or his behavior. Right now, I am sorry I ever invited him to our home or agreed to dine with you, Mr. I'm So Prim and Proper. You acted like an ass, as did he, and I have no words for the woman you were with other than I hope you got your money's worth." The accusations dumbfounded even me. If all of this was, in fact, true, Father had made an unruly mistake and teetered on the fine line of the relationship with his daughter. Oh, my, the most horrid thought crossed my mind. What if she were angered to the point that she moved back to England? If I had a beating heart, it would crush at the notion. I knew, and have always known, the day would come when my princess would leave the castle with her prince, but I figured I still had time to prepare. Father, what have you done?

Father straightened his posture, like a man in charge, but she had dressed him down, and rightfully so. There was but a nub of a leg for which he could stand if that. "Devon, last night was regrettable. I am sorry. I let things get out of hand; my sincerest apologies. It won't happen again, but do not forget I am your father, and you must speak to me with respect and not in a tantrum of disrespect." I couldn't help it; I rolled my eyes in true Devon fashion. Was the man actually going to go toe-to-toe with his eloquent and wonderfully controlled daughter when he had been the one walking out of bounds?

She was mid-stride out of the dining room when she stopped, turned in his direction, and the words hung in the air, just waiting to be spoken. Without expression or inflection, she replied, "Then act like it." That made two times she had crushed him with that command and disdain. Devon turned on her heel and went to her room. Not another word was spoken for nearly the rest of the day. Even I, who had done nothing wrong, kept to myself until invited into her room. When she whispered to me, I was hesitant at first.

"You called, my lovely?" Looking around her bedchamber, I could see she had busied herself rearranging the furniture in the room. Charlotte had been placed on one of the chairs as though holding court. I picked up the stuffed toy. "I remember a time when she was your closest confidante. I would watch you, and it brought such joy to my heart. My dear, you were most precocious with a vocabulary vaster than many adults." I placed Charlotte back in her seat of honor. Devon was examining her reflection in the looking glass; I stood behind her and lightly kissed the side of her face. She giggled and rubbed the spot I'd kissed.

"It tickles, like tiny sparks of electricity, when you kiss or touch me during waking hours. Odd how in my dreams I can feel your touch, your kiss, and even though I know you do not breathe, I can feel your breath, I think, sometimes. I am no longer angry with Father. I think he felt some jealousy or competition regarding Baron. I forgive Father, but Baron is not the person I thought he was when we met and spent time in England. He was polite, thoughtful, and respectful in England, perhaps displaying a want for more physical interaction than I was prepared to yield, but not pushy or anything. Now he seems so common and brash, and I find him revolting. I don't know what to do and knowing he'll be here for another two weeks, I cannot bear the thought." Her eyes cast toward the floor; it was plain as the nose on her face that she was finding herself at a loss. I wanted to say push him to the door and send him packing, but that was the wrong code of form. "Don't you have some worldly advice? What am I to do, Sebastian?"

Devon sat on her bed and watched as I paced the floor. It was something I needed to ponder. I remembered my parents once hosted a family they had known from Boston at their home. I could tell my mother found them less than desirable, and she sorted out some advice to me. Mother was worldly when it was not acceptable for a woman to be knowledgeable, let alone a woman of color. The women were expected to mind the servants and the home, bear children and make themselves attractive and available to their husbands. Throughout the years, I had taken note of the plight of women, their change in roles to family dynamics, and my appreciation of their strength, courage, and wisdom was of particular note.

I sat in the chair adjacent to Charlotte, smiling a fatherly countenance, and softly spoke. "Whilst entertaining a family from Boston, friends we had known from our time residing there, my mother found their ways not in accordance with hers, if you will. She kept a close watch on the servants and ensured everything in our home shone and sparkled. As children, we knew not to touch the crystals on the chandeliers or wall sconces at a young age and never light or extinguish the candles. It was not our place to do such. One of the visiting friends, Mistress Williamson, took several crystals from sconces in the parlor; I suppose she fancied them. She even went as far as to change the candle in one of the sconces dripping wax onto the floor and rug. No one had to say a word in our family or the home for that matter; it was known. Mother invited Mistress Williamson to share in tea. Very politely, she mentioned the wax drippings and missing crystals, merely saying that it had been her failure as a host to explain her expectations of the household. See, she took the responsibility of correcting Mistress Williamson by apologizing for not having had the good sensibility to explain the ways of our home. Her method corrected the problem and relieved the disappointment in Mother's heart, having lifted it into the spoken word. Maybe, you could do the same with Young Baron. Whether he is aware of proper behavior and chooses to be uncouth or an ignorant swine, you will have stated the rules. Use of this method, as my mother proved, enables you to get your point across and maintain an amicable relationship."

Devon smiled brightly. "I could just hug you, Sebastian; you're always one with the advice of a sage. Yes, that is exactly what I shall do. In truth, I had not told him about Father and his proclivity for over-indulgence. I will slam-dunk all the other points as well." I had heard the term slam-dunk on the screen, but it was a most unusual terminology for Devon; I must stay up with the times, I suppose.

My lovely went downstairs in search of her houseguest. He had bathed and dressed more appropriately. Upon seeing Devon, he stood and asked that they visit in the garden. She escorted him to the brick patio in the back, inviting him to sit beside her.

He spoke at once. Obvious from his expression, he was begging for forgiveness. Devon gazed warmly at him with mercy and kindness in her eyes. I'd hoped she had taken my advice in her delivery. I observed from the window as their chat stoked warmer, their body language far more relaxed and revealing. I also detected the calculated twinkle in the boy's eyes, the almost unnoticeable smirk of an upturned lip, and the slight rise of his brow as though a secret knowing. Maybe he had begged forgiveness, but my instinct said his actions would soon play the role of Jack the Lad. He would fight back to earn her trust, and in one of her more light-hearted moods, he'd make advances, one's I myself had made with gullible young ladies.

It would begin with an accidental glancing touch of the breast or a hand placed slightly above the knee, followed by a tiny slip up her thigh. Yes, old chap, I knew all the tricks and moves to wile a young heart into an unblessed bed or unattended carriage. Without either creature comfort, a passionate action with virility against the trunk of an old oak tree could leave a lass filled with excitement. I shook my head at the mere remembrance of such episodes. I had been such a cad, hadn't I, in my misspent youth? Perhaps if I had paid closer attention to my tutors and Father's business endeavors, I could've made more out of my life and not have it so short-lived. Pining for a second chance would not do anything to further my situation. I had begged my Creator to reconsider, to give me a second chance. So far, I had neither slept nor eaten since my last drawn breath, things I had taken for granted in my young life.

Due to the extreme New Orleans summer heat, the young couple quickly retreated inside. While Devon played the part of an attentive hostess, I could see in her mannerisms that her trust had not been restored, and the flutter of intrigue was a faint shadow compared to the vibrance prior to the disastrous night before. In my experience of seeing many people whilst they thought alone and cloaked from prying eyes, I believe his true nature was that of the peacock-haired slovenly pig from the morning, with his cheeky behavior and common tongue. Time would tell, and I would camp closer to the enemy in the corners of his chamber rather than constantly observing my love. Behind the closed door, perhaps I would learn if my assessment of him were true.

Father called Devon to the lounge. "Yes, Father," she said rather coldly. "Is there something you want?" She stood with arms crossed in displeasure.

"Yes, my dear. Please forgive my lack of decency and discretion from last night. I don't want bad feelings to come between us. We've already sustained enough challenges since Mother's leaving and have come such a far way. I can't lose your affection." Anyone with half their sight could see the man was tortured by his actions, and the remembrances were still bitter on his tongue.

Devon knelt at the side of his chair. "I love you, Father, and all has been forgiven. Let us forget the whole debacle of last evening, shall we? I would love it if you would join us for a bite tonight at Mr. B's, that is, if we can get a reservation. If not, we can play it simple somewhere else. I'm quite certain I don't want to be alone with Baron for a few days. He was inappropriate last night, nothing I can't handle, but I want to test the waters to see if it was whiskey induced or if I have read his character completely wrong, in which case this is going to be a very long two weeks." *Bravo, my princess, bravo!*

My essence applauded her elegance and heartfelt intelligence pairing close to Father, who seemed to bristle at the mention of Baron being inappropriate. She possessed much wisdom for such a young girl, but then again, this certainly wasn't news to this old soul. The impact of the night of deplorable acts had accosted me more than I realized, and she'd not mentioned his inappropriateness to me. No, I told myself, it was not my battle to fight this time.

The next few days went without a hitch. Devon was playing the hostess role to perfection, escaping the grasping hands of her suitor. All in all, the boy had been unremarkable and had not imbibed libations to excess. He slowly drank a beer or two but abstained from hard liquor. My stolen moments in his chambers proved uncompelling.

After a week and a half, nearing his day of departure, I had already resigned myself that the lad was suitable for my young Devon as a friend, but clearly not anything more. I watched as he began to pack up his things when his mobile phone rang. He quickly answered, scolding whoever was on the other side of the call. "I told you I would call when I got home. Yes, it's been fun, and no, I have not slept with her yet. Still, a couple more nights left." He chuckled as he ended the call. Speaking to himself, he said aloud. "That deal shall be sealed, however, one way or t'other."

Well, well, I wonder what Devon might think of such a bold statement. I would hold my thought and bide my time whilst keeping a close eye on the boy. He may have heard the tantrum I had thrown soon after his arrival. Yet, there hadn't been a peep mentioned or reference to said ridiculous behavior in any conversations to follow, so my presumption was he'd forgotten all about the spirit of the Hurstall house and guardian of Miss Devon's virtue.

The following day, as Father left for work, Nellie called in, saying she was under the weather and would be unable to work. Feeling confident of the conditions with Devon and Baron of the Brown Nose, he headed off to work. My lovely was still sleeping soundly in her bed, and Jack the Ripper in his chamber. I sat on the edge of her bed, watching as she slumbered. She had a look of peace with a slight smile on her lips, skin soft as the petal of a flower. Her hair fell off the pillow winding around the edge just so. Devon was beautiful, like a painting created by the master Monet, or Rembrandt; a magnificent creature to behold, indeed.

A creak came from her doorway; the swine Baron was awake and entering her bedchamber, where his person was most unwelcome and inappropriate. He came to her bed, and I, a mere foot beside him. The boy kissed her cheek and began to slide his hand beneath her duvet. *Oh, Blessed Bride, Archangel Michael, and the host of heavenly beings*, I prayed, awaken my love before I have to take matters into my hands and have yet another strike on my most miserable essence. *Oh, God!*

Devon murmured, stretching as was her custom upon wakening. She peered through her barely opened eyes, and rather than shrieking or jolting; she whispered, "Baron, get out of my room now." She began to rise, swinging her legs to the other side of the bed, putting distance between her and beast boy. "Don't make me say it again, or you will be sorry. I promise you have no idea."

He stood solidly, glaring, "and just what are you going to do about it? Nellie has called in ill, so, my darlin', t'is just me and you. I will have what I intended when planning a holiday to America. I have tolerated your spoiled childish ways; t'is time you act like a woman." He threw himself across her bed. "Like it or not, I will have my way, darlin', make no mistake." He grabbed for her nightdress as she spun away from his grasp. "Hard to get does not suit you." His eyes had a determined look and one of aggression and anger. "Stop playing like an innocent child. No girl kisses like you do without having had the pleasures of a man. You think I'm stupid?"

As if in slow motion, he lunged at her, and with hands balled in fists by her side, she let out a scream, "Sebastian! Help!" I forced myself between her and the swine making myself to his aware.

Screaming in a higher pitch than my Devon, Baron of the Brown Nose and swine of the Hurstall house backpedaled at a rate of speed I'd seldom seen. "Christ Almighty!" His countenance appeared as one of the animated characters of Miss Devon's youth. It was a sight I would've paid a good price to witness again.

In my sternest tone, I replied, "Not even close, lad. I believe the young lady requested you leave her chamber at once. My advice, continue to pack your things; you are no longer welcome in the house of Hurstall. My darling friend has provided you with a bed, food, libation, tours of this grand city, and been the perfect hostess, and you repay her affectionate kisses by trying to take her virtue by force? If not for my love for her, I would have obliterated you into a thousand pieces. Now, off with you." I could visibly see his body trembling with fear. He made a straight line to her door, and I laughingly appeared in his path and said, "boo!" He shrieked again. I could hear her laugh at my childish absurdity, but it filled my essence with gladness. If I wasn't mistaken, I heard the song of a choir of angels off in the distance. Perhaps, My Creator found honor in my love for Devon, but then again, it may have been a song from my spirit. It was of no consequence as long as my princess was safe. All was well with my soul.

Upon entering the lad's quarters, I found mirth in his hurried attempt at packing. He muttered to himself amidst a few sniffles and maybe a tear. I presented myself and calmly spoke. "Baron, I do not wish to frighten you again, but I feel the need to impart some sound advice. You see, I, too, like you, was too cocky for my own good. I took advantage of a few maidens in my time, acting the complete scallywag. I, too, broke hearts and took liberties, but I never forced myself upon anyone. I suppose I had more charm than you; nonetheless, I was a cad. It all ended when I fell in love, and I fell hard. Our relationship was not acceptable to her parents; they knew I had plucked a few blossoms from the garden and wanted better for their daughter. In this instance with Devon, you have the benefit of being able to return home, but heed my warning, consider your ways." He stood quaking as I spoke, even though I remained calm and reassuring. He managed to hold tightly to every word, nodding as I went along.

"Y-yes, s-sir. Thank you, s-sir f-for s-sparing m-m-me."

The two days passed quickly, and the time had come for Father to return Baron of the Brown Nose to the airport whilst Devon and I had a right ol' chat. She was amused by my instruction to the boy, telling me I didn't have to expend my energy. The names she called him would have made me blush had there been coursing blood in my body. I had never heard such crude words come from her lips. Our feelings for each other entered a new realm of closeness, even beyond my love for sweet Scarlet. Perhaps, I had become wiser and Devon more acutely aware of the world than my fair young angel. Women were far more worldly than ever before, and maybe that drew us like bees to nectar.

A New Realm

While I was delighted the Irish pest was gone and back across the ocean, I knew things would never be the same between Devon and myself. We had sailed past another threshold into a new realm of discovery. What began as my sheer amusement of a feisty eight-year-old child with the most sparkling countenance and demeanor had changed through the seasons; Miss Devon was now closing in on womanhood, soon to be embarking on furthering her studies. We had but this one year left. One thing was for sure, I not only loved her, but found myself deeply in love with her. I knew her feelings were much the same, and throughout my entire essence, I knew it was best to start severing our bond. Maybe not forever, but my graceful dove needed to spread her wings and fly without an old soul anchoring her with fantasy thoughts within the confines of her nest. It was as transparent as the lounge window; I had to distance myself, much as I found the idea more painful than anything I had ever considered. Plunging over the upstairs banister was an action with no thought, only passion; the prolonged sting at the time did not compare to this gnawing pain that would endure endlessly for some time to pass.

I had hoped life would take its natural progression, and while it would wrench my soul, I had predicted I would be merely a stop along her way. It was during these contemplative moments when I'd stroll her bedchamber, admiring her trinkets and browsing her photograph collection, that these rambling thoughts of the inevitability of her future came to the forefront. My favorite photos were of her as a child before the family moved to New Orleans. It made me smile, remembering all those times she'd told me how much I would love England, and from the pictures, I could easily see myself strolling the streets, frolicking with her in the parks, and living in the formality of her life there.

"Sebastian," she called out as she entered the house. Nellie was busy cleaning Father's study, but I found it bold for Devon to call out my name. *Indeed*, I thought, *Nellie would have heard her; regardless, my precious had summoned me.* I rushed to her beckoning call. "If I didn't share my news with someone, I would explode!" She bounced along with her words. "This year in school will be my best; I have a feeling. I have every teacher I secretly hoped for, and to think it's my last year. What could be better?"

I did not think such excitement would come from a selection of teachers. From all accounts, Devon had never had a substandard teacher; no, something was odd about this exuberance. "I'm delighted for you, my dear. I hadn't realized it was of such monumental importance. Perhaps, I've missed something along the way."

Somehow my response left her deflated, making me wish I had made more of an effort to appear just as thrilled as she, even though I was clueless. "Don't you see? For Calculus, I have Mr. Elliott instead of Mrs. Fitzmorris." As she mentioned the woman's name Devon rolled her eyes. I was no more enlightened than when we began the conversation, but she continued. "I have Mr. Peterson for English, Mr. Germain for French, and—" She continued, but I began to see a pattern. I wondered if all of her teachers were men.

"My dear, are all your teachers male? Is this what the excitement is all about?" From my question, she gazed at me as if I had grown an extra head.

112

"Hardly. I have mostly male teachers, which is a bonus for me. Because I am such a good student and so smart, I am fortunate that all the teachers love me, well, except, maybe not Mrs. Cramer, but she's jealous of me, I think." I always knew my darling was opinionated and thought highly of herself. Which she should, but not to the extent I was hearing. From appearances, I think she fancied herself better than anyone else. Such a thought could lead to worry for me because the hurt one experienced when the truth of the matter came to light would cause a torturous tear in her heart.

Once again, an observation from my own overzealous experience in life. At one time, I thought I was a slice of heaven for all who met me. It wasn't until my father pulled me into the lounge by my ear after I made a similar statement to what my dearest had made. He explained that while I had many wonderful attributes and was accepted well by most, I was merely another wonder of the Creator's making and everyone was the same in the Creator's eyes. He found my behavior appalling and distasteful, and quite frankly, he was ashamed of my conceit. I found myself conjuring similar thoughts as my father had once expressed, but Devon was not my daughter, and thus it was not up to me to correct as a parent might, but her words were worthy enough of my comment—later.

Devon sifted through the mail, finding two letters from universities. One was from Boston, and the other from Tulane, a local university down the avenue from home. Whilst being a nosy cad, I'd listened in on the conversations between Father and Devon regarding university plans. Father had strongly suggested she apply at Oxford, where she would be a legacy. Both Mother and Father had graduated from Oxford; in fact, that is where they met. Needless to say, I was dumbstruck and heart wearied by the possibility. My essence tingled from head to toe when Devon showed no interest and made her preferences known. If I'd had a say, Tulane would be the best choice, but I realized there was no room for my opinion on the matter after considering my motive.

Our young lady needed to experience life, and staying home would not truly be of benefit. I watched as she carefully read both letters and took note that she laid the letter from Tulane back on the table and took the response from Boston into her room. I followed closely. She didn't have to say a word; I knew she had made her choice. Our little bird was going to spread her wings and fly. Boston was lovely, indeed, but my memories were from a different era and a much younger age. What it may be today was entirely uncertain, and I had to have faith that The Creator would watch over her.

"Sebastian," she called out, still reading over the letter.

"Yes?" I took form. "Do you have news?"

"Sit by me. As you know, I have applied to many universities and am awaiting a response, but I heard from Tulane and Boston today. Please don't take this the wrong way, but I want to move away from home, if only for a year, so Tulane is in my Probably Not pile, and Boston is a Possibility. I hope you are not disappointed in me."

I smiled at her. No, I wasn't at all disappointed in my cherub. I was, however, heartily displeased with myself for allowing our relationship to become what it had. The bond was all my doing, fulfilling a most inappropriate and regrettable moment of careless curiosity. "My darling, I am not disappointed in you at all, quite the opposite. More than likely, all of your letters will be of acceptance. You are most remarkable. I shall not deny my essence will gravely miss you and long for your visits home, but I've known this day would come. I am most proud of the woman you've become. I always knew you'd be something special." She tried to embrace me, and then we both laughed at the tingles of electricity between us.

A single tear rolled down her face. "I will miss you, Sebastian. You are the best friend I have ever had, maybe even the only friend I've had. I'm friendly with many of my classmates, but I don't have a bond with any of them. Some of the girls have what they call besties, and maybe Claire thinks of me as her bestie, but, in truth, my bestie is you. Too bad you can't come with me when I go. Rather than think of sad thoughts, let's make the most of the time we have. Agreed? This school year has just begun, and there's much mischief to be had." Had I a beating heart, it surely would have been crushed at the thought of my treasure moving away. With Mother being gone and now after this school year, I wondered if Father would sell up and purchase a smaller place, perhaps downtown.

When the Hurstalls first purchased the home, I found it odd that they would want such a large home having but one child. It really was a shame, the house would be perfect for a family with six or eight children, but it always seemed to be small families who bought the house.

Once Father arrived home, Devon ran to greet him. "Oh, Father, it's been a wonderful day. I think school will be smashing this year, and I've already received two acceptance letters from universities. Once I receive acceptance from them all, I will decide which suits me best." Overhearing the conversation, I hoped Father would take the opportunity to talk about her propensity for conceit. It would be much better to come from Father, Nellie, or even regrettably, me, not some unfeeling counselor or fellow student.

"Sounds good, my dear. Devon, you do realize you may not get accepted into all the universities you applied to? Something you must take into consideration; I don't want you to set your expectations too high." She cocked her head with a puzzled look, both eyebrows almost knitting together.

Devon unfurled her brows, righted her head, and quickly responded, "Oh, well, their loss." I felt like beating my head against a wall. What was it going to take for the young lady to understand the world did not revolve around her? I could see Father had the same look of concern I felt.

"Devon, would you like a touch of wine? Nellie can bring in some cheese and crackers; I think we need to talk a bit, my love." Thank Heavens, Father was going to take the bull by the horns, and I could be there to mend the pieces.

"I would love some wine and time with you. We will have to make the most of this school year to hang out, as I will be going away to school, and we won't be able to get back this time."

I pondered how Father would broach the subject without causing too much hurt or instigating a storm. The house was particularly cold when Miss Devon was in a foul state. I had faith in Father. Nellie brought in a bottle of wine, two glasses, and a tray of nibbles. I sat in the adjacent chair, getting ready to watch the show.

They toasted new beginnings and the passing of time. "Devon, I've wanted to speak with you regarding a few things of concern to me, and I'm not quite sure where to start." Father put down his wine glass and steepled his hands, peering over the tops of his fingertips. "Well, I'll just be out with it. I worry about you and your choice of men. Take, for instance, this Irish lad; he certainly pulled the wool over your eyes during your time in England. Otherwise, you would never have invited him for a stay here. Young Wills, well, is just that, young, still quite attached to Mummy. I know you have another love interest, though you haven't brought him around, I can tell. You get the look in your eyes as a young woman in love." She started to interrupt, "No, let me finish, I know you know about sex, and I don't want any details, but if you need contraception, by all means, sort that out."

Devons' jaw dropped, ready to go into combat. Father raised a finger and stopped her. "Perhaps the thing that concerns me the most is your lack of humility. You are exceptionally beautiful, smart, quite funny, and have much to offer the world, but you need to keep your high opinion of yourself, well, to yourself. Nothing is more unattractive or off-putting than a braggadocious, self-righteous, arrogant ass. Remember, there will always be someone prettier, smarter, funnier, and positioned to light the world on fire. Self-confidence is good, and Mother and I have always encouraged it, but conceit and an overfullness of oneself are not a quality, but rather a distraction. Do you understand?" *Bravo, Father, well done, indeed!*

Devon drew a long sip of her wine. Eyes wide as a doe with exaggerated blinks. Was she appalled, hurt, angry, or, God forbid, argumentative?"

She sat quietly as a church mouse for a few minutes. Father started getting uneasy in his chair; I could tell. With a deep sigh, she answered. "Perhaps, Father, I feel like I need a cheerleader, someone rooting for me on the sidelines. You and Mother didn't have time to address most matters with me. Please don't take it as I'm angry; quite the opposite. Because I had to be there for myself, I learned preservation. I would never make such comments in public, but if I can't react with confidence and perhaps airs with you, then who can I?" I could see Father's heart crush, and I, too, felt like I had let my treasure down. I knew I told her often of her beauty, but reflecting on her date to the basketball game, she was in such a twitter over what to wear and how to kiss; shame on me that I didn't pick up on her fear and vulnerabilities. She desperately wanted to fit in, and I missed the signs. My poor, poor child, how many ways had I and Father let her down? Her eyes glassed with pools of tears. Oh, no, no, it would be more than I could bear.

Father ran his finger along the edge of his wine glass which made a high-pitched whine. "Darling, I am so very sorry. I will endeavor to be more aware, but you need to open up to me; I don't have a crystal ball." He looked into the glass and swallowed the lot of it down.

"Oh, and Father, about the 'I'm in love with someone.' Yes, but I assure you, you would not understand. I have chosen to go away to school, and I am aware all the universities might not accept me, but if I were a betting person, I'd say I'll have way more acceptances than 'thanks but no thanks.' So, essentially, I am going away to see if I truly am in love with this certain person and when I am sure you two will meet. As far as BC pills, I haven't jumped in the sack with anyone yet." Father had become unsettled, changing his position like he was on a hot seat.

Food for thought for this old spirit—although only in a dream, had I deflowered my lovely Devon. There was no doubt she was all woman and returned love as much as she received.

Father poured another glass of wine, clearing his throat. "So, I hope I didn't hurt your feelings. I think you are the best thing since sliced bread, and in my eyes, there is no one as beautiful or witty, and I am proud to be your father, my sweet. I am very proud of you, Devon." She set her glass down, got up, and leaned over to kiss Father on the cheek.

"It's all good, Dad. It's time we get less formal in this house. One of the girls from school pointed out that I always referred to you as Father, like that was your name. Some of the girls call their parents by their first name, so I'd call you Ian." His eyebrow went up in disapproval. "Fear not, I think Dad works just fine, just not Father. It feels so stifling. We need to relax some, agree?" Up the stairs, she trotted.

She sat on her bed, flipping through the pages of a magazine. Fifteen minutes went by, and I couldn't take the silence. "Hello, my precious; you and Father had a lovely chat today, don't you think? I heard you mention being in love. Someone I haven't heard of, darling?"

With almost no expression, she looked at me with a cock to her head. "Really? You know who it is full well. Have I not told you enough that you are the man of my dreams? Have I not told you how much I love you? I also know it can't go on forever; well, I suppose it could, at least until I die, but I want to have children, and I am afraid a dreamland affair will not result in pregnancy. I know we can't marry. You can always walk in my dreams when I am here. In fact, I look forward to it." She blew me a kiss with a flirtatious giggle.

Truthfully, I had hoped she would take an afternoon nap. I wanted to declare my love. I lay beside her, wishing I could pet her hand. They were so slender and dainty. Oh, if they could strum my chest, I would surely melt into her arms or she into mine. I found that I increasingly grew angrier with the Creator as the days went by. I knew this was to no avail and would probably result in being tossed into the fiery pits of Hell if I kicked up too much. No, I was acting like a petulant child. I had this beautiful toy to play with, yet I could not touch her.

"Sebastian, would you like to join me while I nap?" She smiled with a glint. I returned a broad smile because there was nothing I'd rather do. She tossed and turned until finally settling in and falling to the Land of Nod. I patted my hair, tugged gently on my waistcoat, and took the plunge.

Devon was sitting on a bench overlooking a quaint river and waving at the occasional passers-by. It was marvelous. As I was getting ready to kiss her, a disturbance rose from the river as a motor-powered boat raced up, drenching us in water. Who was it other than beastly Baron. I stood with hands fisted at my sides. The boy had pushed me too far. I had been benevolent with him, or somewhat. Instead of looking at the situation for what it was, only a dream, I took personal affront and lunged onto the boat. He sped off, leaving my sweet Devon on the bench alone. "Turn this vessel around immediately!" I shouted. The boy laughed at me, and I realized at that very moment I had not changed the slightest in all this time. Because of some maddening machismo, I had lost her and once again lost love.

The boat raced down the river toward a roaring end. Was I about to enter the gates of Hell because of my foolish behavior? I jumped from the dream just before going over the edge as quickly as I could. Alone in the attic's darkness, I noted that I was dripping water all over the floor. Had I misbehaved so poorly that My Creator would truly cast me to Hell? I fell to my sodden knees and begged forgiveness, expounding on all the wrongdoings of my life and afterlife. I didn't hear His voice, but I knew what He expected of me. My Creator, instead of casting me into the abyss, had allowed me interaction of a sort with life. Throughout the many years, I knew where I stood. I was merely an essence of a human but could watch and experience many of the joys of life. Thinking too highly of myself, wanting to cast Baron into the abyss, and taking on the role of an all-powerful being, I stepped way beyond what delighted The Creator. Who was I to think I could punish anyone, especially a figment in a dream? It wasn't even my dream. I overstepped my place and knew I would have to answer for my poor judgment, stripping me of the ability to watch and interact. I was a damn fool.

I had overreached one too many times, and the precious gift of my Miss Devon, my treasure, was removed from me. "Most Benevolent One, please spare me from this misery." In my essence, I could feel His warning. He drew me from my treasure's countenance, and it would remain so, until He decided to place me back, and that was if He ever returned me to her. He

119

might return me through His mercy, but would she even remember our friendship? Would she ever forgive me? Would He erase me from her mind as though we had never met? I was despondent and took my place at the old secretary, still in my wet clothes. I slid a page from the stack of stationary and began to pen a letter to explain to Devon what had happened, but the pen fell from my grasp. I could no longer even jot a word. Silence. I would be in silence. How long would I stay in this purgatory? I had nothing but thoughts of my horrid and irrational mistakes.

In the distance, as though spying through a faraway tunnel, I saw a cloudy vision of Devon as she pushed sleep from her eyes. "What a most peculiar dream." She said. "Why would I dream of Baron? Horrors! He was such a jerk spraying me with water. No Mother again today, maybe next dream. I remember she and I were on the bench together." I desperately wanted to say, 'No, my love, it was I, Sebastian, by your side.' The message My Creator was sending me illuminated that He had cast me into a Hell of sorts without being relegated to the fiery pit for eternity. Perhaps, it would be a penance of sorts. He had not forsaken me. I had nothing but time on my hands to wallow in despair and think. In my mind, I relived each of my misdeeds over and over. My thoughts punished me with constant worry. What if the memory of me was forever cast from my Devon? What then?

I knew time was passing by, but how many days, weeks, or even years had I remained in darkness and silence? The difference between then and now was significant. How fortunate I had been all those many, many years. He had allowed me to break a barrier where I actually found happiness in an otherwise barren existence. Certainly, he would not punish her; she was an innocent. I supposed that one brief scene of Devon waking from her dream was my last observation of my precious treasure. Still, it only led me to know I was no longer a participant.

Benevolence

Years spilled through time in an endless stream of darkness and silence. I no longer heard Devon's voice, and it was maddening. Had she forgotten me? I could and would never forget her; of that, I was sure. I begged His mercy with promises to comport myself as a gentleman. To what avail would it be for the lovely one to remember old Sebastian? The Creator was not allowing the door to open between my permanent state and Devon's life. He was all-knowing of that which was good and fair. Had He, in fact, allowed the door to open between Devon's world and mine, or had I, the insistent cad, forced my only hand and revealed my essence to her? It was sheer depravity.

While stuck within these old walls, with family upon family taking up residence, this old soul was trapped to spend eternity inside the walls of my misadventure. I suppose He could have tossed me to the fiery flames or into a dark, meaningless void with a gnashing of teeth. The big picture presented a most loving, benevolent Creator that allowed me some semblance of happiness watching as the ages marched on. While not an active participant, I could watch and fill my existence, but my insolence and selfishness brought that to an end.

The Creator had struck me deaf and blind to the words, the voice, the actions, and the life of the one I held so dear. There was no need for sadness; I brought the whole demented obsession on myself and had no one to blame but me. What started as sheer delight in the joy of a most determined and precocious eight-year-old child had mutated into an unholy obsession of a carnal nature. Had I just left well enough alone playing the role of a spirited invisible uncle, not a lecherous deviant, then my blissful existence would have been blessed with joy and not isolation and loneliness in a darkened world without light or sound. This was my new eternity.

Then one glorious day, a sound broke through the stillness. How long had it been since I had heard the pleasant melodic song of voice? A bustle of noise filled with squeals and laughter echoed from what I assumed was the front of the house. Was this still the house of Hurstall? In an instant, I recognized her lovely voice.

"Nellie! Can you help me with the bags?" I raced to the front of the house as though driven by madness. To lay my eyes on her beautiful visage would have taken any breath I would have once possessed. It was the voice of my delight, yet she seemed so much older. How long had it been since I heard her delightful voice, certainly but a few days, maybe months? Oh, my, had it been years? The Creator had sanctioned me apart, but it hadn't felt the time it had been. Did my precious even remember me, or had the memory of me been stricken from her mind? Was that, too, my punishment?

"Your father is in the study," Nellie advised. Devon flitted through the heavy wooden doors with a beaming smile across her bowed lips.

She rounded the back of his chair, snatched the papers from his hand, and leaned over, bestowing a kiss on his forehead. "Devon, you are a rascally one. I'm so happy you are home from Boston. I would have been delighted to pick you up at the airport, but you're here, and that's what matters, right? It's been boring as the dickens since you've been away. So much to catch up on, my dear." She plopped in one of the chairs in front of his desk, tossing his papers to him. "I do wish you had elected to walk across the stage. We could have made a big to-do with a party, your mother, Sean, Grandmother, and the entire English family coming to Boston to celebrate."

She smiled. "It was just as I wanted, no fanfare required, but you'll never guess who I ran into at the airport. Jeffrey Charles. Remember him? He has grown to be quite a specimen. I barely recognized him. He asked me to dinner sometime and gave me his number. I may ring him; after all, we've known each other for eons." My, my, ol' Jeffrey Charles. Now that was a name I hadn't heard in years. My Devon seemed somewhat taken aback by the lad. Interesting. From my memory, he had been nothing short of a nuisance. Yes, he had. Her first comment was referring to him as a baboon. I chuckled inwardly. Then, the boy dared to steal a kiss. Hmm, I wonder what Miss Devon might think now about a stolen kiss. My fears were coming to pass as it was apparent she had no recollection of our entangled bodies or any remembrance of me. Just as well, I supposed.

"Dad, I need to unpack my things; I'll be down straightaway. I wanted to tell you about my marks and life in general at school, but we have stacks of time." She kissed him again and ran up the stairs. Kicking off her shoes, she threw herself across the bed. The first thing she grabbed was her diary stuffed with all the letters I had written her. She eagerly read each one. "This is so strange. I wonder why I created this person—Sebastian, the man of my dreams— it's so sad. I was such a lonely little girl, but these letters seem so very real, as though it had been a deep, forever kind of love. Poor Father, he spent a bloody fortune on therapy to erase my imaginary friend." While she continued to debunk any notion of a real person, she continued to pour over the letters. "And yet, I still feel a tug on my heart, like one of a passionate love, one to withstand the ages." She sat quietly in full contemplation. I could see the cogs whirring in her mind.

Tightly closing her eyes and gripping her knees to her chest, a whispered word escaped her lips in an almost dreamy fashion. "Sebastian."

Oh, dear, what was this spirit to do? I knew full well what I wanted, but what was the prudent act? I begged my Creator to please direct my path. I did not want to make the mistakes I had made previously, yet I knew if I answered, I would eventually succumb to her luscious lips—kisses I had been denied, in supposition n'er on four-plus years. I still loved her deeply. Perhaps, if we stayed mere acquaintances and not ventured down the path of lovers, it would fair well. I begged for an answer, yet I knew this was a fine example of free will and what a mockery I had made of it before. I could no longer deny myself. "I have missed you, my precious."

Devon cocked her head to the side. "Sebastian?" She glanced around the room. I took form. "They made me believe you were an imaginary friend, but I knew somewhere inside you had been real. Is it truly you?" She stared through me, her vibrant violet eyes filled with wonder.

"Yes, it is I, my love. I have missed you terribly and cannot believe the Creator has permitted me to hear you and see you." This time I would make it right.

"There is so much we need to catch up on. Do you remember our last meeting?" Did I remember? I still reeked of moldy wet togs, the only smell to penetrate my oblivion of punishment and a staunch reminder of the ills of my past. I merely smiled. There was no need to re-hash my near derailment and plunge into Hell forevermore. "For the life of me, Sebastian, I cannot recall our last encounter. It was as though you were a memory from childhood, yet I have felt an unrequited burning of passion. None of the boys from school quite held the flame properly, leaving me wanting. Not that you are interested, but I have had a couple of boyfriends, but none fit the bill if you get my drift." She smirked as she raised her eyebrows. Must I sit through this diatribe of inadequate lovers, boys missing the mark? "I feel as though you and I had a remarkable love affair at one time, or did I imagine that as well?"

This line of questioning left me in a quandary. Part of me, perhaps the machismo side of my once manhood, wanted to expound on what a fabulous love affair we indeed had, but then what was the kind thing to do?

"My dear, we, indeed, shared in a kiss. I believe it was when you were going on an outing with a beau at the time and felt unprepared for a kiss, but you were a quick learner, and that was about the extent of our dalliance. Otherwise, you and I have shared a love that transcends a physical nature. It is far grander and would pale any romance. What we have is so much more." This explanation perked a fire in her eyes and was just what was required to fulfill her heart's desire.

"Yes, I remember now. Ours is a love for greater than a lifetime, and you are correct when you say it transcends the emptiness of sex. One day, my Prince Charming will come along, and it will all be perfect, but until then, I could not ask for a better friend, and I am happy beyond belief that you are not merely imaginary. If I remember correctly, I cannot hug you as you are mere air, but I did read that I thought you were a spider on my back at one time." Before I had a chance to pull away, she reached out and wove her arm through mine. "Yes, it tickles like a thousand tiny electric impulses. Now I must go down and see dear old Dad." She quickly popped up and made her way. "We'll talk later. I have so much to share with you, my friend." In a flash, she was gone.

After a lengthy conversation and a few glasses of wine, the two left for dinner. Before leaving, her phone rang, and it was none other than Jeffrey Charles. According to their conversation, the young man would stop around for a visit the next day. At least, I would be able to lay eyes on the once villainous scoundrel. I remembered all too well that my precious cherub had a somewhat questionable discernment in the ways of the male species. After scolding myself about letting the past go and starting afresh, I looked forward to reserving judgment for myself. Perhaps I was as versed in scoundrels because I had been one in my youth, and as the adage went, 'it takes one to know one.'

I'd forgotten what a busy person my Devon was. Between tidying her room, giving a hand in the kitchen, and making countless phone calls, she barely had a moment of solitude or reflection. As when Devon was a young lady, she still went to great lengths to select the perfect ensemble to entertain her guest, this time Jeffrey Charles. No sooner had she bathed, dressed, and coiffed her splendid mahogany locks than the front chimes rang. She ran to the door and opened it with glee. "Come in. It is so good to see you; what a fun thing it was running into you at the airport." She chattered away, the young man unable to get a word in edgewise. Slowing the pace, he took her elbows and stood directly in front of her.

"Devon, take a breath. Yes, it was stellar seeing you, and you are lovely as ever. When we first spoke, I was afraid you'd scarcely remember me, and I've long since dropped the double name to my parent's disdain; please call me Jeff." Well, I must say, I was impressed. He was a fine strapping man with a face for the screen. His demeanor was kind, and I could see sincerity reflected in his eyes. He well might do for my princess. Maybe this was her Prince Charming—grumble. With all my chagrin set aside, I actually felt happy for my treasure. He was a man I could see sipping Port with or sharing in an in-depth conversation. He was intelligent, engaging, and had a genuine interest in Devon and not just a heart full of lust. I was none too naïve to expect that impulse didn't lay deep within him; how could it not?

I found myself becoming quite fond of Jeffrey. He was good to my precious love appreciating the unique parts of her personality and sharing the same reverence for her as I. He knew how to speak to her in such a manner as to keep her in check.

He had graduated from a prestigious university in Massachusetts and was furthering his academics at Tulane. It had been mere coincidence that he had run into Devon if one were to believe in coincidence, which I, personally, did not. No, The Creator meant for those souls to reunite and fall in love. As far as this old ghost, I held no resentment or disdain for the young man.

My sweet would beckon me a few times a week, and we enjoyed conversation, games of chess, her experiences outside of the house, and the changing of the times. On the rare occasion, we would watch the television.

One of those nights, she was full of questions. The man and woman on the screen had a challenging love story that ended tragically, which stirred thoughts of my sweet Scarlet.

"Sebastian, you've never told me how you died. I know you took your own life, but what drove you to such desperation?" The question had finally come, so I answered her truthfully, and for once, I felt comfortable speaking of that horrid night.

"My dear, I was madly in love with a fair young lady, Scarlet Monroe, daughter to Elias Monroe, a well-to-do figure in the community. He had vast inherited wealth, whereby he could live in the city and oversee the business ledgers without residing in the country. His family owned sugar cane plantations near the French settlement in southern Louisiana. Scarlet was betrothed to Theodore Arnault, owner of the largest coffee enterprise in New Orleans. He was considerably older than her, easily thirty-plus years her senior, and the arrangement was not to her liking, but back then, ladies did as they were told, no matter how seemingly perverse. This house, your home, belonged to the Monroe family back then.

"She had the most beautiful golden hair, and her eyes were like sparkling blue pools of water." I closed my eyes, letting my mind recall her beautiful countenance and lovely ways. I could still feel her kiss on my lips as though it were yesterday. I sighed, "She and I fell madly in love. We kept our love a secret. The servants in her home knew of our clandestine courtship but wouldn't say a word as they also knew her father's heavy hand. He was a terribly wicked man. They knew she was betrothed but also how we loved each other. The servants often let me in the back door when her parents were off socializing away from the house.

"It was on one of these nights when I was visiting that her demise and mine occurred. We were in her bedchamber in the throes of passion when one of the servants burst into the chamber, announcing her parent's carriage had just returned. We had enough time to dress, but when her father demanded her presence, well, it was evident she had been up to something—her hair was disheveled. He raced up the staircase, grabbed her by the shoulder with one hand, and slapped her harshly with the other; I could clearly hear the strike. I desperately wanted to go out and stand up to him, but I knew it better to stay hidden in the chamber. Ezekiel, the servant, tied the bed linens around me with plans of letting me down through the window. I lost all sensibility when I heard the repeated strikes to my Scarlet. I came out of her bedchamber mad as a crazed wild animal. I was just in time to see the blow that sent her falling down the staircase to her death. I went blind with rage and threw myself off the landing. The linen caught on the railing, and I suppose the weight and trajectory of my leap were enough to snap my neck, ending my young life. I believe Scarlet strolls the Heavenly streets of gold, and because I brought about my own demise, I am forever bound inside the house. It could be worse." Devon was tearful and put her hands to her face.

She sobbed, "Utterly awful. What a dreadful man; I hope he's burning in Hell. Sebastian, I am so sorry. Thank you for sharing your story with me; I know it had to be painful to re-live. Maybe one day, God will let you join Scarlet."

"My sweet," something like chills ran up my spine, "that has been my prayer for over a hundred years. I am happy that you have found true love with Jeffrey. Have you ever told him about old Sebastian, your ghostly friend?"

"I've tried and started to, but where do I begin? I don't want him to think I'm crazy. Most people don't believe in ghosts, and he might think I'm not the girl for him." I wanted to tell her that if he were, indeed, the man for her, he'd give it a listen and trust her words to be the truth. "According to my diary, you made quite a disturbance in the attic for everyone in the house to hear, and yet my father sent me to a therapist to address my imaginary friend. I was too old to have such, so I think, for now, I'll keep you a secret. I hope it doesn't offend you."

I assured her I was not offended in the slightest. It conjured up memories of Franklin, the older man I had visited for years. His family and the servants all would comment about his senility behind his back and laugh at him. The man was hardly senile; he was sharp as a tack but had the gift to see me, yet not understanding my condition being dead. So, I could see where Miss Devon might be scrutinized harshly, and that certainly was not a thought I relished. It shocked me that Father acted as though he didn't remember the commotion I had caused in the attic during my outburst when the Irish lad visited Devon. The boy had been such a thorn in my side and a swine to boot.

Our lovely conversation came to an end when she retired for the evening.

I wondered what her dreams were, and although a risky proposition, I decided to take a stroll and have a look for myself. In the dream, Devon and Jeffrey were in his vehicle, and while I was interested in their conversation, I was more intrigued by the sights and changes of the city. Jeffrey drove to the business area as I remembered it, but it had vastly changed. To my shock, many of the establishments were bawdy with a clientele full of whiskey. I was appalled to see how the crowd attired themselves, certainly not as we did when we went into town. The area was immensely different, and I didn't care for it in the slightest. Jeffrey steered the car into a dank opening, stopped the vehicle, and another fellow greeted him, and it appeared the young couple was on the move, so I had to follow. The crowds were truly uncivilized, knocking into one another without so much as an apology. Jeffrey took my dearest's hand, fought the sea of people, and buffered her way along the street. I followed close behind, although I desired to perhaps gape at the atrocious behaviors of those on the street. Some young couples were in passionate embraces against the walls of establishments; men were urinating in front of anyone who glanced their way. The whole scene was despicable. I was pleased to see that Jeffrey was a gentleman, and Miss Devon held herself with class. They entered a place I had heard mentioned before, Pat O'Brien's. The lad led them to an unoccupied table. I had entered her dream; thus, I followed her or had to step out. It wasn't as though I could meander at will. Part of me would've liked to walk around nosing into the atmosphere, but being only an invader of her dream, I did not have that luxury. So far, I had managed to avoid her taking note of me. I knew all I had to do was speak, and I would have her attention.

She whispered to Jeffrey, "Can I tell you a secret? Just listen until I finish; then you can ask questions, okay?"

"Absolutely, Devon; what is it?"

"First, let me ask you, do you believe in ghosts?"

Jeffrey laughed, "seriously?"

"Yep." She watched him.

He looked at her with all sincerity. "No, only because I have never seen one, but I know a couple of people who swear they've seen them. I don't know what to believe."

"So, do you think they're crazy, or do you believe them?"

"I have no opinion; I guess because I don't care enough about the subject. If there are ghosts," and he made an odd sound, "then I truly won't believe it until I see one for myself."

Rather than introduce myself at the time, I chose the better part of valor and stepped out of her dream, thankfully unnoticed. Should it be my mission to teach the boy or let him go on without a clue? After all, it was Devon's dream, and she needed to make the decision.

Our friendly existence continued without anything remarkable. We were two friends with a closely held secret. I must admit, I did experience an ache of sorts knowing that Devon had not remembered our most intimate moments. I missed that aspect of our friendship as I still very much loved her.

Courting My Sweet

The courtship of Devon and Jeffrey grew more serious. She had confided in me her desire to marry him and had high hopes that a proposal was in the near future. While I wanted the best for them in the relationship and for my lovely to have her heart's desire, I knew marriage would parlay into my treasure moving out permanently, only to visit on occasion. Surely, Father would sell the house, being the only one to take residence in the place. It would inevitably feel hollow and a haven for endless echoes.

The festivities of Mardi Gras were in full swing, and Father hosted several parade parties. On this one particular night, Jeffrey imbibed a tad too much, and Devon insisted he spend the night. While she was bathing, my young friend Jeffrey invaded her chamber, saw her diary on the shelf, and took liberties he had no right to take.

Donned in her nightdress, she returned to her chamber to find Jeffrey nose-deep in her diary.

"What do you think you are doing?" She stood with her back arched and hand on her hip, obviously outraged. "That is my private diary, not meant for the eyes of others."

With a slight slur to his speech, he responded with arrogance, "I should think I can see anything of yours by now. I've seen everything else." He gave her a snide grin. That was more information than I wanted to hear, but, nonetheless, his behavior was atrocious, full of drink or not. "You have some answering to do, I should think. If you are to be my wife one day, then I need to know everything about you, and we should have no secrets. Do tell me, who is Sebastian? You told me about the Irish guy, and I knew about Wills at the time and the few boys you dated in college, but nothing quite as serious as this Sebastian fellow. From your writing, it appears that the two of you are still in some sort of relationship. Well, say something, Devon." He was angry, and I sincerely hoped I did not have to interject.

"Firstly, I do not appreciate you going through my things, especially my diary. Oh, and by the way, my purse is off-limits as well. Regarding Sebastian, let's just say you wouldn't understand. He's a very dear friend and has been since I was eight. You have no need of insecurity when it comes to him—

He took a few steps toward her. "Why? Does he not like women? If he's so important to you, I would have thought you'd introduce me to him, or does he not know about me, like I didn't know about him?" The argument was getting heated, but it was something they both had to see. If their love were true, then a disagreement would have no bearing on their feelings for each other. It was apparent both were hurt to the core. I wanted desperately to show myself and get it over once and for all. My presence would most definitely clarify many things. "Well?"

"I told you, it's not like that, and I'm not so sure you would want to meet him given the situation." She walked up to him and held out her hands for the diary. "Think it over, and you decide if you want to meet him. If so, I can arrange it like that," and she snapped her fingers. "But, be forewarned; it will be an experience like no other, I assure you." He handed over the diary but clasped my letters tightly in his hand. "The letters as well."

Jeffrey began reading one of my letters aloud. "Deeply devoted, my dearest—what kind of man speaks like that, I ask you?" He continued to read in a mocking tone. It took all I had not to present myself. How dare he mock my words of love.

"That's it, Jeff; I've had enough and remember you asked for it." He started to turn his back on her when she called out to me. "Sebastian, please show yourself." I knew it was unwise, but I could not deny her; I would not deny her, especially when she needed me. I took form, and I could feel my essence buzzing with energy. If I wasn't mistaken, I believe my essence took on a glow; how distinctly unusual, I thought.

Jeffrey stood with his mouth agape, eyes nearly popping from his head, but he didn't back down. He stood his course, which earned favor with me. "I am Sebastian, sir. And while you find my formality a source of mockery, I assure you, my treasure, Miss Devon, finds it heartwarming and exciting." He moved in my direction. If the lad thought he would intimidate me or attempt to do harm, he would soon learn that the game was not played that way. He put his hand out as though to shake mine as one would do whence introduced to another.

His voice wavered; it was more than apparent he was taken aback. "I suppose this is the part where I say; it is a pleasure to make your acquaintance, sir." While he tried to hide the tingling from attempting to shake my hand, I could see the sensation register on his face. "I'm sorry if I insulted you, and I sincerely hope you do not hold it against me." He looked at Devon, "and I'm sorry I pried into your diary. I now know why you've asked that question of me. Up until this very moment, I had not encountered a—" he looked in my direction for the correct terminology for my presence, he shrugged his shoulders, "ghost?" I closed my eyes and nodded in affirmation. "I'm not sure what I should say from this point on."

I could tell he was dumbfounded and tried the usual things one would do upon meeting someone, but it was beyond reach at that moment. I jokingly responded to his confusion. "We could always play a game or two." I smiled broadly in jest. "Or I could leave you two alone; I feel certain you might have things to discuss. Jeffrey, for what it's worth, whence in the home of Hurstall, you can call upon me at any time, and I will answer unless I am with my most precious one." I gracefully bowed at the waist. "Devon, my darling, I shall take my leave now. Is there anything you desire?"

Her eyes sparkled, and her lips turned upward in a bow as she spoke. "Not at this time, and thank you for being so, um, you. Goodnight." I abandoned my form but wanted to hear the following conversation; I was most curious and admittedly a nosy cad. What sort of impact had I made on ol' Jeffrey?

Feeling a green cast of envy, I watched as he embraced her. "Devon, I will never look at your things again. I'm sorry for crossing the line, but in the same breath, blown away to meet your friend. From his attire, I would guess he lived in the late eighteen hundreds and from a refined, well-to-do family. While I have a tinge of jealousy over your closeness, I can't help but be fascinated by him and look forward to speaking with him again. I'm anxious to hear his story. I guess I better get to bed before your dad finds me in your bedroom." He briefly kissed her. "I love you, Devon, and always have." It was a sweet moment of sheer sincerity, and I found myself cheering for the lad.

As sleep swept over Devon, I found myself compelled to walk in her dream. To my pleasant surprise, I found her sitting on the very bench she had conjured so many times before. I cautiously approached. "I can feel you, Sebastian; please sit." I did as commanded. "Thank you for being so kind to Jeff. I want you to know something, and this is between us only. While away at college, I dreamt of you often. I called you my Mystery Lover." She giggled and hid behind her hands. "I wondered where I had seen you or if I had completely made you up. Watching you with Jeff tonight, a vivid dream came to mind—one of a scandalous nature. When I was younger, you said you kissed me to show me how. Did you demonstrate any other intimacies, you know? Did we make love?" Her head cocked ever so slightly, and a sultry smile crossed her countenance.

Was she genuinely asking, or was she attempting to seduce me? I was determined to walk away from such dalliances. It was unhealthy for both of us, and I had to close the door on such conversations, much as I wanted to hold her, kiss her, and take her as mine. She belonged to another.

"Oh, my darling, your college dreams were your own creation. You know very well I cannot leave this house, so I couldn't possibly walk amidst your dreams."

Devon stopped me. "I know it wasn't you, but I find it amazing I remembered you in my dreams but not when I was awake. I'm not asking you to do anything you are uncomfortable with; I'm just telling you about my memories. Of course, if you would like to kiss me, I wouldn't put up a fuss."

I had to set aside my desire, and there had to be some standard between Jeffrey and me. That would not be the action of a friend, and if I were a living, breathing man, I doubted young Jeffrey would invite me into the boudoir of his intended. I put myself in his shoes and had this same situation involved Scarlet and not Devon, I knew full well my thoughts and perhaps actions would scarcely resemble a gentleman but a territorial brute. I had to break the trend in our conversation; it did not take a seer to know the path we were about to take. I needed to step out of the dream and post-haste; I knew my resolve was weak, especially when it came to my lovely. "You are most stunning tonight, Miss Devon, but I fear I must bid ado. May you have a restful night's sleep." I took her hand and kissed the top of it before stepping out of her dream.

The following months served to strengthen Devon and Jeffrey's relationship. He had called upon me several times. It had been a very long time since I had male company; the last interaction was when I scared the bowels out of Baron of the Brown Nose. That wasn't entirely true. I remembered offering advice to the Irish scoundrel; before that, my last male interaction had been with elderly Franklin. And that had to be nearing seventy-five years prior. I missed the old codger when he passed away. I had been by his side and saw when an angel of the Creator came to bring him to Heaven. How I wished he had gathered me unto his bosom and taken me too; alas, I remained alone with Franklin's empty shell until the servants found him. There hadn't been mourning or tears; I think I was the only one filled with sadness.

Jeffrey was always delving into what things had been like in my time. He touched a couple of times on my circumstances but avoided the hard questions. I suspected Devon had told him the sordid story whilst on an outing. I followed the lad, my presence unknown, into Father's study the evening he asked for Devon's hand. Father was rather shocked, evidently, asking for the hand of one's daughter was becoming an obsolete practice, and I couldn't help but think how unfortunate. Father offered Jeffrey to take a seat. I do not believe he had any idea of the precipice fastly approaching.

"Mr. Hurstall, I am here to ask for your daughter's hand in marriage." He sat with a straight back but held a humble countenance. Had I been Father, I would have found Jeffrey a man of worth and a suitable husband for Devon. Had Scarlet and I survived long enough to marry and fill a house with children, life would have been grand. I would have found a man such as Jeffrey to be a stellar candidate as a husband for my daughter.

Father questioned Jeffrey with a stern look and manner, which surprised me, I must add. "When are you thinking of proposing? I know you have a part-time job, but you're still in school. You do know that once you finish law school, there's no guarantee you'll get hired? Many law school graduates are waiting tables or bartending."

I admired Jeffrey's assurance. Despite how Father had spoken to him, he answered with poise and conviction. Well done. "To answer all your questions, I have a job offer for when I graduate; not making much at first,

136

I know, but I see the growth potential, and as far as when I'll propose, I have a few ideas. I thought maybe in May, commemorating our running into each other in the airport, or perhaps a holiday like July 4th with the fireworks on the river in the background, or taking her to the Bahamas for Labor Day and doing it there. Do you like any of those ideas?"

The world had changed, for sure. An engagement in my time was far more formal, everything arranged by the parents of the happy couple rather than the bride and groom themselves. In fact, the bride had no say in any of it. More often than not, there was an arrangement between the young woman's father and someone he thought suitable, even if the man was two, maybe three times her age. There would be a matter of the bride's dowry in exchange for a good station in life. Yes, things were most definitely different. Jeffrey had been thoughtful in the scenarios for the proposal, and it tickled what would have once been my beating heart. He loved her, there was no doubt, and while Father was skeptical about Jeffrey's ability to provide, I had complete faith in the young man. Exciting as it may have been, all the discussion of marriage presented a dismal scenario for me, one where Father would sell the house after Devon married. Hmm. This old spirit had to accept the inevitable and get on with the thought of a new family. Grumble. Grumble.

The proposal did not occur in May, and before I knew it, the 4th of July was days away. I pondered whether my treasure would get her wish then. Jeffrey waited for Devon in the lounge, so I took the opportunity to chat with him and pry, nosy cad I was indeed.

"Good evening, young sir." I didn't mean to startle Ol' Jeffrey, but he flinched nonetheless. "Sorry, sir. I did not intend to give you a start. I have not had the pleasure of your company in the past week and thought to check in on you. All well?"

His shoulders relaxed, and I felt an honesty about him. He spoke to me with respect but warmly as a friend. "Yes, better than all right. The only word that comes to mind is splendid. I believe I picked that up from you, Sebastian. If I tell you something, can you keep it secret from Devon?" I nodded with a raised brow. I, the picture of secret-keeping, would be the ideal subject to trust. "While Devon and I watch the fireworks near the river, I plan to ask her to marry me. Do you know, when we were kids in elementary, I knew then I would marry her one day? Isn't it great when dreams come true? Even though she hasn't said yes yet, I feel confident she will."

And there it was, right from the horse's mouth. My Devon was going to become his wife. Yes, I was jealous but happy for my sweet, even though I knew she burned with passion for me and that love could only be unrequited. As they say, that ship had sailed. "That is exciting news, and I am happy for the two of you. There is nothing better than when a dream comes true. Your secret is safe with me."

I knew the July 4th plan was going to take Devon by surprise. From our conversations, she had indicated there might be a proposal at Christmas or New Year's Eve. I relished the thought of her giddy girlish excitement. I had managed to keep the green eye of Envy at bay. My sentiment regarding Miss Devon had not changed, and I still longed for her kiss. I imagined myself on one knee, holding her hand, eyes locked with hers as I asked her to become my wife. In some ways, I was grief-stricken but managed to put my feelings aside and bask in her happiness. We shared a bond unlike any other, and I had to console my sadness and appreciate the reality.

July 4th finally arrived, and I wished most deeply that I could have left the house to watch his proposal, but such was the way of my situation. I'd have to patiently await her return home.

A most fervent cacophony came from the front of the house. Jeffrey tried his best to subdue her boundless energy and verbosity but relinquished the reins knowing his efforts were merely an act of futility.

"Dad, you must come at once." Father had arranged a small gathering of his friends and associates to celebrate July 4th. While it wasn't such a thrilling day for an Englishman, it was a time to gather with friends and be social. He broke away from a conversation rushing to her. "Look, look," she held out her dainty left hand. "Isn't it the most beautiful ring you've ever seen?"

Spying over Father's shoulder, I admired the ring and had to give the lad credit. His taste was exquisite, and the ring on her lovely, tapered finger provided a compliment. The diamond and her hand were a duet in perfection. I moved alongside her for a closer look, and I guess the closeness in proximity to each other brought about a shiver to her body, and the hairs on her arm prickled slightly. Yes, my lovely, I wanted to say, I will always love you, but I am thrilled to congratulate you on your engagement. Perhaps later, at bedtime, she would summon me and reveal every moment of the proposal. Tides had shifted, and I no longer dropped in her bedchamber to visit; I waited for her to call me and found that she was too busy or not inclined to spend time with me on some days.

Near one in the morning, the small crowd dispersed, each going to their home bidding farewell and an abundance of congratulatory remarks on Miss Devon's engagement. After the excitement, Jeffrey prepared to leave about a half-hour behind the group of guests while my lovely had retired for the night.

"Excuse me, Mr. Hurstall, sir, if it's okay with you, we won't have the actual wedding until after I complete school, so the engagement will be a little longer than what most people expect, ya know; it'll be more than a year away, closer to two."

Father put an arm around the young man's shoulder, "Jeff, whenever is fine with me. There is no rush on the date." The two sat and chatted while I eavesdropped on a not-particularly-interesting conversation. I hadn't gone to the rafters as I felt an impending beckon from my treasure; surely, she would want to fill me in on every minute detail.

I heard a faint whisper of my name. Was I willing the voice, or was it real? I gambled. I appeared in her bedchamber. "Did you call me, my dear?"

"Only ten times, Sebastian. Can a ghost lose their hearing because, I swear, I've been calling you a lot lately, and either you are ignoring me or can't hear me?" Her face was most stern, and I felt as though I had been reprimanded. She sat up in her bed, waiting for me to come nearer.

"Tsk. Tsk. If I had heard you, I would have responded. Perhaps you are not whispering loud enough. I wasn't sure if you were calling me just now, but I hedged my bets. Now that the telling-off is over, did you want something?" She proudly displayed the diamond ring. "It is lovely, and it becomes you and you it. When will the nuptials be?" Already knowing the answer, I didn't want to attract attention to my caddy eavesdropping.

Ever so nonchalantly, she responded, "Who knows? I'd say at least two years. Truthfully, Sebastian, I don't want to move out of the house. I know we'll need a place of our own once we're married, and I don't look forward to it. I'm definitely not moving into Jeff's apartment. Would it be awkward for you if we moved in here?"

I wanted to ask if she purposely attempted to crush me or if her question was honest without intention. As fond as I was of Jeffrey, I did not want to be privy to their marital bliss. I had to fight my envy when they shared an intimate kiss. No, even though I wanted to be the bigger man and give the pretense that their relationship bothered me not, the truth was it rendered me grief-stricken. Why wouldn't my merciful Creator relinquish the chains binding me to this earth and whisk me to Heaven? Would that day ever come?

Unforgiving Freedom

I watched as the cast of sunlight changed with the seasons. While some of the foliage and trees were cloaked with colorful leaves, seasons were delegated more by festivity than actual changes in the temperature. New Orleanians defined Fall as Football season, even though the temperatures could range from blazing hot to freezing cold, depending on the day or even the time of day. The other seasons that came to mind: Mardi Gras and Hurricane, were not the typical Winter and Summer.

My treasure and her beloved, Jeffrey, were happy as two fleas on a long-haired dog. He was ever-charming and patient with her almost tidal mood swings. There were moments when I wondered if my lovely suffered from emotional maladies or was merely a victim of the female flux. Whatever the slant of the case, I tipped my hat to ol' Jeffrey. He was level-headed and reined her in gently.

While I'm certain there had been other disagreements between the two, this day was the first I bore witness to, and I did not care for it one little bit. They were standing on the landing, my least favorite place in the entire Hurstall mansion. Jeffrey was too close to the banister as far as I was concerned. The argument became quite heated. My lovely had dug her heels in, and when that was the case, there was no changing the course.

"Jeff, I am not, under any circumstance, moving into your apartment. What about the *not*, don't you get?"

He thumped his hands on the railing in anger. "And I am not going to live in your father's home. What part of my reply don't *you* get?" I despised him leaning against the banister, especially in the precise place where the sheets had caught, thereby breaking my neck. A cold sensation bristled up my spine, a feeling I had never experienced and hoped never to repeat. In an instant, I understood my Creator was warning me of impending danger. And, perhaps, it was in that inkling when He imparted my course of action, for I certainly had never had the plan of action before, even as a thought.

Still, with raised voices, the two of them heatedly argued neither one relenting. In an instance, there was a loud cracking and a duet of screams. I swooped beneath Jeffrey as his body crashed to the floor. I was merely air and had never been able to assert affection or touch anything of flesh, only inanimate objects, and yet, I had seemingly cushioned Jeffrey's fall. It was almost as if the Creator, Himself, had reached down His mighty hand for a cloud-like landing.

The most incredible situation presented itself. Whence Jeffrey, shaken with a pounding heart, moved and stood, my essence was part of him, almost as though locked inside his body, unable to remove myself. I, as it felt, was the only essence inhabiting his body. Where had Jeffrey's essence gone? I was at a total loss for comprehension. Had my Creator given me a second chance at life inside the body of another? Had I become that other? Was I no longer myself? As I stood, I turned toward the immense looking glass on the wall of the grand entry.

Before me was the body of Jeffrey, yet clearly with my eyes and mannerisms. Yes, my Creator had given me a second chance. I suddenly found myself weeping for my lost friend. Jeffrey's essence was gone. Perhaps he was walking the streets of gold and might find my Scarlet, perhaps entrusting her with the wonderous experience our Creator had provided. I fell to my knees, thanking Him for this chance at life and promising to make it as rich and complete as possible, staying on His path.

My lovely had raced down the stairway, sure-footed to my side. We looked at each other in the reflection of the looking glass. I didn't have to utter a word; Devon knew right away.

She took my hand and looked into my eyes, "How? I know it's you, Sebastian." She threw her arms around my neck. She whispered, "Where is Jeff?"

Quietly I answered, "Perhaps walking the streets of gold. I don't know, but our Creator is merciful."

I had no idea how much time had elapsed, but Nell ran to the grand foyer. She looked up at the broken banister, then at me. "Dear Lord, Jeff, I heard the crack of the wood all the way in the kitchen. I'm amazed you're alive, and it appears you suffered little, if any, injury. Praise God. It's a miracle." She looked toward the Heavens and crossed herself. I knew I held myself differently than Jeffrey and my eyes were golden, not blue. Had no one looked that closely except my treasure?

I took Nell by the elbow. "Truly, it is a miracle, indeed. Ever so sorry to have frightened you."

I made haste back to Devon and looked deeply into her eyes. "Of course, my love, we can stay here after we wed. That is if you still want to marry me." She nodded, both of us with tearful eyes. Nell called Father, told of the horrible incident, not mentioning the heated argument prior to the calamity, and said she would have the carpenter come to the house at once. The fall had also cracked a few of the spindles, leaving a rather significant gap in the railing. I went directly, moving the hall table to block the opening lest someone stumble.

We retired to Devon's room, where we cried in each other's arms. I would miss my friend and was sure my treasure would mourn the loss; it was to be expected. My only experience with the outside world had been through her dreams; I was well behind the mark for proper behavior. What was their relationship like outside these walls? There was so much I did not know, and I felt sure I would appear a bit daft when there was much I needed to understand. Would Devon be able to teach me, to prepare me for the world beyond the house? Could I perhaps feign some sort of memory loss or odd behavior from the fall? I would need to defer to Devon on these matters. And then what about school? The questions flew through my head in a constant stream, perhaps more like the torrent of a swollen river. I no longer fit into the outside world, and while I was of an above-average intellect, I might seem a complete buffoon. I didn't know Jeffrey's friends, or his parents, or anything except those of the house of Hurstall. All my prayers for a second chance had been answered, but as the adage goes, be careful what you wish for: you might just get it.

"Sebastian, oh, I mean Jeff, I don't know that I will ever be able to call you Jeff. How did you end up in his body? I think Jeff would have died from the fall."

We lay in her bed, her arm across my chest. How many times had we been in the same position; she wishing she could feel me and not the tingling buzz of my essence. I cleared my throat of a balled-up wad of emotion.

"I imagine he would have met an untimely demise. Moments before the crack of the banister, I experienced a strange sensation, almost as though I knew there would be an impending danger that I needed to handle. I knew my essence was void of substance, but for some reason, I wanted to try and block his fall, so I came between his body and the floor. The weight of his body seemed to engulf my spirit, and Jeff's soul disappeared just as quickly. I've heard the term spirit possession, and I can only surmise that was what had occurred. My dearest, my head is filled with rambling thoughts, and while I have prayed for another chance at life, there is a world of matters I had not considered. I am utterly unprepared for what lies beyond the front door."

Devon coughed out an attempt at a giggle through her tears. "You silly man, you will adjust; I know it." Her body shuddered with slightly controlled gasping sobs. "I feel heartsick and empty since the catastrophe. There were many moments he and I shared, as I am sure you and Scarlet shared. My memories are all that is left, it seems. If you think about it, even though our relationship is completely changed, I am confident we shall conquer the awkwardness of it all and create new memories. What's bothering you?"

Where could I possibly begin? The list seemed endless. For lack of a better explanation, I simply replied, "I am not Jeffrey. I don't speak like him nor comport myself in the same manner. The English language has changed with the times, as have the rules of living that one takes for granted. Was he close with his parents? What did he call them? What were his favorite places to go, or what were his favorite meals? I do not know how to drive a motor carriage and am not familiar with the rules whence on the road. What about school? Although I was more unaware than aware of it at the time, the law has also changed. What agreement was Jeffrey's understanding with the law firm, the one that offered him a position following the completion of his studies? You see, my darling, it is as though I am born again and rendered impotent as a small child. Do you understand my struggle and apprehension?"

Devon rose and stood by the window, gazing into the back garden. It twigged at that very moment. I wanted to sit in the garden with her, filling myself with air and feeling the sunshine on my face. I walked up behind her, cradled her waist, and gazed out the window. "Let us go into the garden. It will be the first time I have been out in the fresh air in over a century and a half. My emotions, my sweet, are frayed and shaken, like Father's celebratory libation."

"You mean martini. I can clearly see where your expressions and word choice might be an issue or sound an alarm that something isn't right with you, that is, you as Jeff. Maybe I could come up with a pet name—sweetheart, baby, honey, or maybe, my love."

We walked down the stairs, through the house, and out into the garden. The sun on my face was exhilarating. The fresh air felt intoxicating. "Devon, this is wondrous, and as far as pet names, the only one that could be tolerable is 'my love'; however, you cannot call me that all the time. No, we shall adjust to calling me Jeff. I'll have to stay on my toes when it comes to speaking with Father. I'm afraid Mr. Hurstall will not roll easily off of my tongue."

Devon took my hand and drew me to her. My heart, yes heart, filled in a most magnificent way. I could feel the flush throughout my body. "S-Jeff, let's practice. I'll say something, you answer me, and then I'll update your word choice. It'll be fun. As far as all the other questions, Jeff and his parents don't speak very much and never of any serious matter, requiring merely a 'yes or no, sir,' maybe a thrown-in 'uh-huh,' 'yep,' or 'nope.' He and his dad shake hands, never a hug, only hugs for his mom. We can always fall back on the head injury from the fall."

My girl had it all planned perfectly, but I knew the reality, and things were going to be more complicated than she anticipated. More than anything, she needed to grieve the loss of Jeffrey and not sweep those feelings under the rug. If not, they would manifest in other ways. While, yes, Jeffrey's body was present, his soul, persona, and entirety were gone. We could play the head injury for so long, and that was it. I smelled the flowers, sat on the grass, lounged back, and gazed at the sky, which looked like something out of a painting. Big, billowy clouds suspended above.

Devon laughed at my wonderment but richly rewarded me with a kiss. Her lips were delicate and delicious to kiss, even more so than in her dreams. "Let's take this easy, Devon. While I want nothing more than to kiss you, touch you, and hold you, we need to take it slowly." While I knew I had not slept since my death, I somehow felt this was a dream, and I would wake to find myself still entombed in the house.

"It's time we go to your apartment so you can see where you live. I will teach you how to do the laundry and maybe go for a ride in Audubon Park, where you can practice driving the car, not whatever you said. Let's get going. There are places to go and people to meet, oh, and lots of new words!" Her emotions rolled like the waves of the sea, up one moment and down the next. I imagined this episodic behavior would reign for some time.

"Splendid, I suppose," I answered.

"No, you say, 'cool.'" Her bow-like smile beamed with enthusiasm. I wondered when it would all come crashing down, and the reality of the situation would sink in. Would she still want to be with me? Would she somehow blame me? It was his fiery temper that caused the banister to break. In truth, I had never seen him act in such a manner. Oh, I knew how enraged Miss Devon could make one feel, but either there was something more to the conversation, or there was an unattractive streak in Jeffrey I had not witnessed.

"Cool," I responded—what a strange answer— if I were to be a modern man, I needed to sharpen my use of modern lingo. I remembered listening to the radio with old Franklin. The tone, speech patterns, and inflections of all the voices that came across through the box sounded similar—nasally with clipped words. Yet, Franklin spoke slower in a more refined gentlemanly manner and didn't stoop to casual slang like the voices on the radio.

Devon and I went to Jeffrey's home. Upon entering, I could see why my lovely hadn't any interest in residing there. Couldn't say I looked forward to spending much time there either. There was one living quarter, a small kitchen, a bedchamber, and a privy. Judging from all the books scattered on the table, I surmised my friend was serious about championing his education and future. "My dearest, I see your reasoning in the desire to reside at your father's home. In your father's house, the two of you could have had the entire third floor to yourselves." She sighed at the mention of their wedding. Casting her eyes to the floor, she nodded. "My sweet treasure, there are bridges of grief you must cross, and it is with the hope you and I can build a life together." Again, she nodded. Was the reality beginning to sink in? My heart broke for her as I gazed upon her distraught posture. Quickly moving to her side, I was able to catch her as her body began to collapse to the floor. I lowered her gently, pulling her close to my side.

"Jeff's lease is ending, and I thought he should move into our house rather than sign another year's lease. That's how the whole argument started. I should've just let him sign the stupid lease, but I thought it would be throwing money away. Living with my father, we could've saved money for a down payment on a house of our own. He's usually sensible, but he was being hard-headed and unyielding. If I could do it over again—" she began to sob.

I thought on the subject for a moment, quickly racing through the positive and negative outcomes of a decision I was about to suggest. "Devon, perhaps I should gingerly broach the subject with your father regarding the sensibility of the situation. He might find our suggestion prudent and well-thought-out. Do you agree, or should we not mention anything of the sort? Be mindful, my love; it would be most inappropriate for me to dawdle in your bedchamber." I sat her down and quietly pulled up a chair for myself to the table filled with books.

My eyes dropped to a page of Jeff's notes, and there was yet another difference between Jeff and myself. The elegance of penmanship from days gone by sorted out those of breeding and those of not. Having watched Devon scribble in her diary, I already knew this was a change in the etiquette of society. The Hurstall family was of substantial pedigree, no doubt—judging from Grandmother, their ownership of the mansion, and magnificent furnishings. Mother and Father held Devon to high standards, which spoke volumes of her breeding and class.

While one might think the owners of the St. Charles mansion were and had always been people of intelligence, high standards, and moral code, such was not the case. Soon after Franklin's passing, a family moved into the grand house that lacked the civility and upbringing to live in such a marvelous and stately place. Fortunately, their residence did not last long, and they sold up quickly. I was delighted to see them pack up and move elsewhere. Not that it mattered to anyone but me; I disapproved of them living in the mansion. I suppose death had not imparted humility in me, and I found myself still an arrogant cad. However, this last set of circumstances humbled me in a most extraordinary way.

Devon asked me. "Should we speak to him together, or would you rather talk to him man to man?" I looked into her eyes, and for once, and I mean once, I saw a lost little girl. Even as a child, she concealed any sense of weakness or vulnerability. In retrospect, I could think back to a few circumstances where it would've been most appropriate for her to feel at a loss. She had cried and felt sad but maintained control. Yet, my treasure always took the road of the brave and outwitted her opponent or the situation. She wanted my guidance.

"I think you and I should go in together and speak with Father, I mean, your father. We will stand unified, and he will know that neither you nor myself have manipulated the other." I felt a bolster in my chest, and as I rose, I noticed a boldness in my posture. I had always held myself well, but this was different; it felt more authoritative. It was good to be a man, to feel like a man, and not some old soul left to walk the halls in perpetuity. Was I gaining some of myself back, or was this Jeffrey helping in the transition?

Devon clutched onto me. "Hold me, S-Jeff, for as long as it takes. My knees feel weak, and my heart trembles, almost like a child in a frightful nightmare. Are you having trouble deciphering the madness of it all? One minute I feel like myself; the next, I realize the situation. Then, maybe as a protective mechanism, I revert to the sense that all is well." She cocked her head to the side, gazing at me through her always inquisitive violet eyes. The question was an interesting one. Since the accident, what seemed eons in the past, yet merely hours, in reality, I, too, had gone through a palette of emotion. What does one say to such a perplexing situation? I held her close, cocooned in my arms, hoping to pass on a feeling of security. Together we would forge through and find peace.

"My treasure, would you take me to a church? I need to confess, and I'm advising it may take some time. My sins have been great, and many, to say the least. Now that I've seen Jeffrey's apartment, we must leave, but first, I'll grab his tablet as a template to practice his writing and make it my own."

Devon gathered a few items; I speculated things of a dear remembrance while I stowed Jeffrey's notes in a valise by the door. I couldn't help but notice some of the items she collected were belongings of hers I'd seen before. She had spent quite a bit of time in the apartment—not mine to judge. Looking around the room as though taking the measure of the place, Devon said, "We will have to come back and box all his things at some point, at least before the lease runs out. I'm sure Dad wouldn't mind us moving his few bits and pieces into the attic. Most of the furniture came with the apartment and isn't his or, I should say, yours." She took my hand, and we left. Devon placed all her treasures in the back seat of the carria—no, car.

We drove to the church to find confession was in session. Fortunately, we were the only two people in the church other than the person in the confessional and the priest; I assumed hearing someone's confession. Sitting on the pew beside my beloved, I was utterly mesmerized by the beauty of it all. I humbly looked up at the crucifix near the altar and gazed at the beautiful stained-glass images. The statue of the Blessed Mother was pristine, every detail finely sculpted. I remember hearing talk about the building of the church and how magnificent it was; it was truly breathtaking. I hoped there wouldn't be anyone coming behind me. I also thought it a good place to speak to the priest about the happenings of the day. Perhaps, even though I doubted it, he might have some explanation. He would not be able to see me in the confessional; thus, I might maintain some anonymity. The thought crossed my mind that he might want to get a good look at the mentally deranged person to report the incident to the local authorities. My confession would hardly be of a standard nature. In the midst of my thoughts, the confessional became available. I cleared my throat and looked at my darling as I got up, smiling at her as I entered.

Thus it began. "Forgive me, Father, for it has been many, many years since my last confession." I went through the list of my sins which included everything from impure thoughts and lying to fornication. "With the nature of a confession being confidential, there is a subject I wish to confide in you and ask your guidance or opinion." He told me to continue. "Father, what I have to say will defy anything you may have ever heard. I'm warning because it will take an abundance of faith to believe." Once again, he told me to continue. "You see, Father, I was born in the year of our Lord 1852 in Marseille, France. My family moved to Boston when I was a babe in arms, then moved to New Orleans following the War between the North and South when I was fifteen years of age. My family, while being of color, were educated and well-heeled." I ended the story with my death in 1873 and the nature of my demise. I painted my life after death with broad brush strokes, explaining the unnatural obsession with Devon, of course, not giving her name, and then the eventuality with Jeffrey.

I asked how such a thing could happen and, going forward, whether it was wrong to proceed in life as the person whose body I inhabited. There was silence from the other side, and I was waiting for the door of the confessional to spring open, but to my utter surprise, his response, whence it finally came, explained he had heard a similar story when he was a young priest. His answer to my ponderance about how to proceed was simple; God had given me a second chance. Our Heavenly Father was the one who saved my soul. Perhaps because of the heroic act, my Creator saw it fit for me to live. Ours was not to question why but to live a life according to the will of God. He then said he would like to visit with me again and hear a more detailed accounting after giving my penance. I left the confessional and kneeled at a pew close to the front. With the utmost heartfelt prayers, I served my penance. I did not want to leave the church. At that very moment, I realized my love for Devon paled in comparison to my love of The Creator. My decision was made; I would meet with the priest again.

Devon sat patiently waiting for me. I knew patience was not one of her strong suits. As I got up, I saw the priest from the corner of my eye and went straight to him. "I would very much like to speak with you again." He smiled and asked me to follow him. I waved to Devon, beckoning her to come with me. She was by my side in a flash. We followed the priest.

An hour later, Devon and I headed back to the house. As suspected, she was a mass of questions, which I diligently and honestly answered. I thought it best to tell her my decision—I would remove myself from law school and start a path in Theology, not wanting to be a priest but perhaps, a university professor or spiritual counselor. I didn't know exactly what, but I then put the question to my lovely. Did she still want to marry me even though I was not going to be a lawyer?

Father was home when we arrived. He came directly to me with an emotional greeting. "Thank God you're not injured, although I cannot for the life of me figure out how you survived such a fall and then not even have a scratch on you. I'm overwhelmed by the thought." His eyes glassed over, and indeed, he was overwhelmed with emotion. He stood and placed a hand on my shoulder, shaking his head in disbelief at the near tragedy. I thought, *Oh, sir, if you only knew.*

Devon greeted him with a kiss on the cheek. "Dad, S-Jeff and I would like to talk to you about a pressing matter. I know the wedding isn't for a while, but Jeff's lease is over in a month, and rather than re-up or find another rental, I thought he could maybe store a few things in the attic and move into one of the bedrooms on the third floor. It's vacant as you know and it would give us a chance to save money. We could even live on the third floor until we saved enough for a down payment on a house. Think about it; you don't have to answer right away." She pleadingly smiled.

"Why not? And since you'll be living here, Jeff, please call me Ian. Mr. Hurstall is way too formal." He smiled at Devon with a wink. "Sorry, Jeff, that's an inside joke. Devon has accused me of being too stiff and formal at times. I'm afraid it might come from my English upbringing, but she certainly has become Americanized with her expectations and speech. She's anything but formal. Choose any room on the third floor that suits you, but I must warn you, there may be a ghost up there."

I wanted to say, "not anymore, sir," but refrained. I felt this move might help with my transition from being myself to Jeffrey. Every detail was perfect whilst in the house; outside of the house was a picture of great contrast. Time, once the enemy to my soul, was now a friend and would shape that which was yet to come. What would the future hold?

Epilogue

Being Jeffrey was more of a challenge than I would have ever suspected. In all honesty, while I wanted Miss Devon in the most rudimentary way, having her was a completely different proposition. Patiently she caught me up on the ways of the current world, incessantly correcting my gentlemanly expressions and even actions. There were some things so ingrained in my nature that she would have to accept them, such as holding the door open for her, pulling out her chair for dinner, assisting with her outerwear, and the use of ma'am and sir.

As planned, I moved onto the third floor of the Hurstall home. Everything in the grand old place was of second nature to me; I had resided there for what seemed an eternity and would have been, except for the benevolence of my Creator. I would not fail Him again.

Whilst Devon craftily attempted to catch me in the midst of changing; I managed to avoid her wandering eyes and hands. Nothing was more divine than her kisses, and natural as it was, I desired her in every way, but I determined I would not fail in my endeavor to please My Creator, and I requested our amorous feelings placed on hold until the nuptials.

"OMG, Sebastian, this is the 21st century, and people do not wait until they're married to have sex. I mean, when you were Jeff, it never seemed to be a problem. I don't know why you are so modest; I've seen you naked many times before. Consider that." She stomped her foot down.

I held my ground. "I think not. Just think how euphoric our wedding night will be. All the mysteries will be solved." I broadly smiled.

Devon turned on her heel and made her way out the door. Just as she was passing the threshold, she turned to me. "I think my dad knows something is up with you. As much as you try, your old-time words slip out. He's far from stupid and quite astute at picking up on nuances."

Still waiting for privacy to change my clothing, I posed the question back to her. With a smirk, "Would you have me tell Father, darling?" If steam could have escaped from her ears, there would have indeed been a mist enveloping her.

"Do as you please." She stormed off.

How I missed our intimate conversations in her chamber—we had supposition after supposition. We were far closer when I was in the spirit world. I must admit, I wanted my cake and to eat it too. Life would have been complete if I could have had the best of both worlds. It certainly gave me much to ponder. I was not "Jeffrey" in any way, shape, or form, and perhaps because of trying to fill the shoes of Jeff, which I could never achieve, both my treasure and I found a monumental struggle. Even though I meant it mischievously, the suggestion of telling Father might be the answer, and we would no longer have to live in pretense.

My mind, consumed with thought, embraced the better part of valor, and I trotted down to Devon's chamber. I knocked a few times, and she finally answered. My heart broke as I saw her eyes filled with tears. I embraced her as tightly as I could without causing harm. I had to tell her my plan and if Father chose to throw me out on my ear, so be it.

I used one of the terms I heard Jeffrey use, hoping to bring a smile to her face. "My holy hotness," she looked up with a smile. "I am going to take the risk and tell Father about the situation. I feel it only fair to him, to you, and me. This existence I have now is almost worse than being a lonely,

154

trapped spirit. Gather the letters and your diary, and join me. I believe we both could use a brandy."

Devon grabbed a Kleenex and dabbed her eyes. "While I love your bare chest, Sebastian, may I suggest you put on a shirt if we are to speak with my dad." While in her scant nightdress, she reached for her robe.

After asking her to wait for me, I returned to my chamber and fell to my knees. "Please let me know if I am doing the right thing. Oh God, I am dreadfully afraid. If this is indeed Your will, let it be done."

The faint outline of a man began to come into view. If my eyes were true, the vision was Jeffrey. "Hello, Sebastian. First, I appreciate the effort you made to save my life, and while I'm not sure why your spirit transitioned into my body, I know we both have the best interest of Devon at heart. I miss our friendship but know one day we will meet again. I believe Ian will come to understand the situation, but I feel part of your and Devon's awkwardness is y'all are trying to make you into me, and that won't work. Be yourself, my friend. In her diary, Devon often said you were the man of her dreams—be that man. Perhaps, things happened as they did because it was how it was supposed to be. It's not ours to question why Sebastian."

Still on my knees, he put a hand out to me, indicating that I should stand. "Please tell me we did not change places. Are you trapped forever to roam—"

He shook his head from side to side with a warm smile. "No, my friend. I have been walking the streets paved with gold amidst the sound of heavenly song. We shall meet again, but you must return to yourself and not try to be me for now. There's nothing you can do with the outer shell, but it is one greatly admired by Devon." He grinned, and his appearance faded away. Quickly I clothed my naked chest and met Devon on the landing.

I could hear Father talking to himself as he often did whilst doing his work. His words were more of mutterances than clear, concise thinking.

Clearing my throat and giving the door a light rap, he looked up. "It is getting late; I was just winding up for the night. Is there something I can do for the two of you?"

I thought *on with it*, drew the chair back for Devon to sit, then proceeded myself. I gathered all the courage I could muster and began. "Ian, while this may be awkward, I have something I feel is essential for you to know."

He interrupted and looked at Devon, "Are you pregnant?"

I was aghast. "No. No, sir. Nothing of the sort. Before casting judgment, please listen to everything we must tell you." I began to unfold the story, starting with their move into the mansion. He listened intently and may have even held his breath at one point, but he understood the words we were saying. As I told the story, Devon moved to his side, laying the letters in a chronological pattern. With a few interjections and confirmations from Devon, I spoke for well nigh two hours, stopping only for a heavy pour of brandy for the three of us. Given the news and the subject of the story, I thought Ian handled it beautifully. He acted as though he understood, didn't interrupt with questions, and appeared to accept it all.

Ian rocked his chair back with a smile. Slight crevices formed on either side of his eyes. "Quite a tale there, you two. The funny thing is my mother told me on several occasions about a spirit dwelling among us. Hmm." He took a lengthy draw on his brandy. "I vividly remember the loud banging and thuds when Devon's friend from Ireland was here, although I tried to pass it off as too many things in an old attic, but I knew." He nodded his head. "I also felt that whomever the spirit was, it was protecting you." He pointed to Devon. "After the accident with the stair rail, I could tell something had drastically changed and found I was having a hard time saying your name. By the way, what is your name?"

"Sebastian, sir. I hope you will forgive the deceit and charade. It is quite a leap of faith to believe our story."

The three of us glanced at each other, and then Ian placed his attention on the letters I had written. He was quiet as he read but would give an uncontrollable melancholy smile now and then. "You have been a good friend to my daughter, sir. I have no doubt that you are in love with her and will make a fine husband for her. From this point on, I shall call you by your name as I'm sure there are many alterations in your lifestyle that will require your concentration. Your name need not be one. Are the two of you still planning on getting married?"

Devon moved closer to his side and hugged him. "Yes, Dad, good God, yes."

"And Sebastian, are you going to move into religious studies instead of law?"

I know my countenance was gravely serious, and I meant every word I said. "Yes, it is my desire if it fits into your approval; otherwise, I will stay the course of law."

Father threw the remaining swallow down his throat. "I only want what is right for you. I'm not so sure that Jeffrey was called to law, but I was supportive. You, sir, I believe, have a call. Now, I want to know your story in its entirety."

Where else should I start but the beginning? I poured Father another brandy and advised him to settle in comfort that I, indeed, would tell my story, no detail untold. He was fascinated by my life, chuckled at my silly boyish antics, clearly understood I had been a randy lad, and then showed sadness, even anger, at the hard part of Scarlet's death. He laughed aloud when I told him of some of Devon's actions in the privacy of her room and how much I adored her love of Charlotte and the adventures they went on in her mind. He could see the blossom of love I held for my darling Devon. There was admiration for my attempt to save Jeffrey and a crystal-clear vision of the trials I had becoming the one I was not. All in all, while trapped for more than a century and a half, I gleaned enough from each of the residents to mature from a scandalous twenty-one-year-old lad to a man of profound wisdom. I was no longer trapped in limbo; in all His benevolence, my Creator arranged for our story to end happily ever after.

Many Thanks...

To my husband, Doug, who tolerates my long hours of isolation, all the while cheering me on and listening to the chatter about my characters and their plights.

To my children for inspiring me to write a teen-friendly story that their children will be able to read.

To those of you that follow my writing, I can't begin to thank you enough for the support and for making me feel like the real deal. Spread the word, the more, the merrier.

To Paige Brannon Gunter for her eye for detail, objectivity, and appreciation of my stories. What would I do without you? Thanks for the suggestion of the Epilogue; it made all the difference. I loved the picture of your childhood teddy.

To G. Lee and K.N. Faulk for storyline guidance, and to that note, the editing bubbles have decreased in the extreme. Is this old dog learning new tricks?

To Julie Agan for enjoying my characters, for sharing her thoughts on my books, and for an outstanding job with grammatical corrections. I love your questions from a reader's point of view.

Reviews are appreciated. The more reviews, the better my ratings! Please drop by my website corinnearrowood.com. Sign up for my quarterly newsletter and freebies.

Other Books by the Author

Censored Time Trilogy

A Quarter Past Love (Book 1)

Half Past Hate (Book 2)

A Strike Past Time (Book 3)

Friends Always

A Seat at the Table

PRICE TO PAY

Coming in 2023

Leave No Doubt

Fit the Crime Series

The Innocence Lie (Book 1)

The Identity Lie (Book 2)

About The Author

Born and raised in the enchanting city of New Orleans, Corinne Arrowood brings an authentic voice to her writing with passion and love. The marvels of the city, both with the good and not-so-good nuances, lend to the colorful characters and experiences discovered in her books. Her descriptive writing submerges the reader into the heart of the city…the people.

From the Heart of the Author… As always, I wish you love.

Touch base with me at corinnearrowood.com